Sara Hoyt

Her Mother's Daughter

By Pam Stevens

To the Love of my Life

You have always been there for me!

For better or worse

Always cheering me on!

And

Thank you to my

Children and Grandchildren

Your cheering and support

Also help me to keep the faith.

Prologue

The Reluctant Courier ended with Sandi and Steve getting together. They had a daughter who is now a young woman. Steve has done his best to prepare her to be a survivor and not a victim, but who can be prepared for what she faces?

Contents

Chapter One

He could see her in the distance, sitting so still that she almost appeared to be part of the rock she was sitting on. The breeze caught her long blond hair, lifting the light strands and whipping them around her face. She was so caught up in her thoughts she did not seem to notice.

Sara sat there contemplating the last few days. Her whole world had been turned upside down; part of her felt numb, almost separated from it all. It seemed like a bad dream, one she would wake up from, and her father would just walk through the door like the whirlwind driving force he was, laughing and joking, demanding the best from her, all the while being her strongest ally and best friend. Part of her hurt so bad that she felt like crying forever, because she was not so sure he would ever just walk back through the door, yet part of her was still convinced he was alive and on the move, maybe hiding, maybe hunting; but why? *Who would he be hunting or who want him dead?*

The nightmare had started the week before. She had been in London and Germany, meeting with different software writers on behalf of the business. She stopped. Maybe it had started before that, when her father had suddenly needed her to go to London to attend the meetings. Had he known then; had he sent her there, to get her away? There were way too many things that did not make any sense. She had never been the one to meet with the software writers. Her dad had always done that part himself. Usually he did not even do it in person; usually it was only the first couple of meetings in person, then he would set up a secure line and they would communicate by a computer conference. Only not this time, this time he walked into her office, laid a plane ticket on her desk, and said she needed to be on a flight in a matter of a few hours. There were not only a couple of new people to interview, but she needed to meet with a few of the regulars and make sure they were on track. He had handed her a stack of files. "Study these while on your flight; you'll be up to speed and ready," he told her. Why hard files, why not computer files? When she began to protest, he looked her in the eye and very seriously said, "I need you to do this for me, Sara. Please don't ask any questions, just go." Then he smiled that beautiful smile that always lit up the room for her and said, "You'll wow those computer geeks, and they won't be able to work for a week after they lay eyes on you!"

"Dad," she protested. He had always complimented her on her looks. She did not think of herself as all that great, but then she had always been way too busy to notice the stares from the opposite sex. She was slender, without being skinny, with long blondish hair and blue eyes that made anyone who looked into them spellbound. He was sure she would be the prom queen in high school, but she did not even go. He was sure she would be swept off her feet in college, but he wasn't even sure she had gone on a date. The truth was she had fallen for a guy in college, but he was what her dad would have called a player, so she never told her dad about him; she killed the relationship and never looked back. When she brought someone home to meet her dad, she wanted it be someone he would approve of and love as much as she did, someone who would be like the son he never had. *Now that might never happen,* she thought. A single tear overflowed and traced a course down her cheek before her hand wiped it away like it was a bothersome fly. There would be plenty of time later to cry; right now she had to think. There were more questions than answers. Some things were seemingly so small and insignificant, yet maybe they were important. Why did he send her with hard files and not files on her laptop? Big things, like who would have wanted her dad dead, and why, and did they succeed or not?

It was frustrating beyond belief. Everyone seemed to think her father had died while being attacked by a robber at his own front door. No one but her seemed to really believe it was premeditated murder; they all seemed to chalk it up to a robbery gone wrong. Of course, not one of them could explain where his body was. They said the perpetrator took the body and hid it somewhere. She knew the last message she had from him was different, that he was not himself; he was in what she jokingly called his "spy mode." She knew in her heart he had been in a super watchful frame of mind, and it would not have been easy to take him down or even get the jump on him. She had gone to the police station earlier and tried to convince them they were overlooking something; it was like talking to a brick wall. No one would listen to her. They were convinced she was just an upset daughter who did not want to accept her father's death. His body would show up, they were still investigating, she just needed to be patient; they would solve his murder.

"What now?" she asked herself over and over. "Where do I start?"

"One step at a time, lay it out, mind map it." She could hear her dad's voice almost as if he were sitting next to her. Whenever she had a tough project that she felt overwhelmed by, he would tell her, "One step at a time, lay it out, mind map it; it will all fall into place."

Off in the distance she could hear her name. She looked down the beach. Clive, her cousin, overweight and pimply faced, was trudging along the beach. Out of breath, he called her name again. "Sara," he wheezed before bending over, hands on his knees, trying to catch his breath. There was someone vaguely familiar with him. She stood up in one fluid motion, skipped down off the rocks she had been sitting onto the beach below, and reluctantly began walking toward them."I won't give up, Dad, I will find out what happened, I promise."

"Detective?" She made the one word sound both like a question and a statement. She remembered seeing him yesterday morning when she arrived home.

"Could we have a few moments, alone?" He nodded to her still wheezing cousin.

"You go ahead. I'll just head back to the house," her cousin managed before adding, "Sara, there's an attorney, Harry Reed or Reese or something like that. Mom said he came to read the will. You will be right back, right?" He seemed to be recovering.

"Tell them I will be there in a few minutes, "she replied, turning away to walk back toward the rocks.

"Mom said you should hurry up. They're waiting for you," he called after her retreating back.

Sara stopped and took a breath before turning back to him and coldly closing the conversation. "I am sure they can wait a few more minutes before knowing what my father left them; a few minutes won't change anything." Adding under her breath, "Other than my state of mind."

You don't remember me, do you?" The man in the suit inquired

"You look familiar, but no, not really. I believe I saw you yesterday morning."

"Paul Jensen."

"Of course, I am so sorry."

"No worries, I think we only met once or twice. Your dad was my mentor; without him I would probably have ended up in jail, or worse. He helped me to become what I am today, a captain in the local police force after a stint in the Navy. He was the best thing that ever happened to me. I met you once when you were about fourteen or fifteen, you had just beat the pants off a bunch of Navy NUBs on their own obstacle course. Your dad was really proud of you."

Her eyes lit up. "I do remember meeting you, but you have changed some. I thought you looked familiar, "she exclaimed before asking, "You heard I was at the station this morning?"

"I did."

"If you knew my dad, then you know what I was talking about! Oh; and I am sorry."

"What for?"

"I thought you were a detective; you weren't wearing a uniform."

"I used to be a detective, before becoming the chief of police that is, but I am here on my own time right now. I do know what you were saying about your dad; I have to admit I was more than a little surprised by the scene at your house. It didn't really fit with the man I know. I wanted to talk to you about your visit to the precinct today," he began. "I overheard your conversation. I would like to help you, but I have to say there is not even a whit of evidence in that direction." She started to protest, and he held up his hand. "Why do you believe your father is still alive? What makes you so sure?"

"It's not just one thing, it's a lot of little things; things that didn't make sense until this happened, but now they do, well, sort of."

"Can you list them off for me, but first, he looked at where they had walked; they were back to the rocks where she had been sitting "is there somewhere quiet we can go?"

"That is why I walked back here. Do you know how hard it is to listen in with the ocean noise in the background? Here it is a constant sound. Something about the waves and the way the cliffs are, it almost echoes back. Dad used to come out here with business associates and stand right here by the cliff to talk. He helped develop some of most sophisticated security software in the world. He would always tell me, 'Don't say anything on the phone, or in an email that you don't want the wrong person to hear or read. If you want privacy then talk here in the middle of nature.' The sound is a steady roar, enough to make sure we cannot be overheard."

He was surprised instead of the ebb and flow of the tide and waves, the noise was almost constant."Wow, this is noisy, but oddly I can hear you just fine."

"The acoustics here are weird." She acknowledged before returning to answering his question. "One of the reasons I know that either my father was premeditatedly murdered or is still alive and on the move is that my house is bugged. I don't know by whom or where they are listening from, but I do know it is bugged, and I think I am being followed."

"How, what makes you think that has anything to do with the robbery?"

"I don't think, I know," she interrupted as calmly as she could. She felt like screaming at him, but she knew he was really trying to help. "The day before, he said to me on the phone, 'No matter what happens, remember I'll always love you Stix.'"

"I remember he called you Stix. He said it was because you were as skinny as a stick!"

"Yes, but he hadn't called me that in years, and he had never said 'no matter what happens' when signing off a conversation."

"What would he say?"

"Things like, 'love ya, see you soon'; 'love ya, be safe.' Not once in all the years of saying goodbye to me had he ever said 'no matter what happens.'" Her voice trembled as she was finishing, and her eyes glistened with unshed tears.

"Did you ask him what he meant? I'm sorry to make you go through all this again, but . . ."

"No, no, it's alright," she interrupted, waving her hand. "I am glad to find someone that's willing to listen, and not blow me off like some sort of idiot. I did ask him what he meant. He stumbled and said something like, 'It's nothing, ah. . . just a rough day, I'll tell you about it when you get home.' Then there was the fact that he sent me away in the first place. I had never done that type of trip."

"What'd you mean?"

"I never met with the programmers. Dad always did that and almost never out of town. He would fly them in or create a secure connection, where he could see them and they could talk, but not in person; he would communicate with them and wait for the results. Look, I know it sounds like I'm overreacting, but I know there was something wrong, the way he sent me out of town, the way he was acting, not exactly nervous or upset, just watchful, like he was looking for something, waiting for something to happen. When I did report to him about the meetings, he was distracted, like he wasn't really interested, like maybe the meetings were not really all that important."

"So who would want to," he hesitated to say kill or murder, "who would want your father out of the way?"

"I don't know, but I do know someone did. You know, Dad was a retired Navy SEAL. He was also a congressman; and before that he also did work for the FBI and the CIA, and quite frankly I don't know who else; or what all he did, but I do know he would be very tough to take down. Whoever did this would have had to have planned and worked out the details, and even then, things might not have gone the way they planned."

"So if that's the case, why wouldn't he have called the police, brought us in to help, hell, brought me in?" He asked, sounding as frustrated as she felt.

"That would depend on who he thought was behind the attack. He may be trying to draw them away from here, from me. He maybe hunting them, or God forbid, he may really be dead." Her voice shook again at the last.

"One more question, what's the deal with the attorney and his will? How can he read the will? I know you don't have a death certificate yet, we don't even have a body; hell, we haven't officially declared him deceased."

She smiled ruefully and nodded. "That's probably just my aunt's version. I think Harry is just checking in on me. I'm sure Dad gave him instructions on what to do if he was ever incapacitated, what was to happen, who was to be in charge and take care of his business."

"That is you, I would think," he responded.

"Probably; maybe it is, not that I really have more than a minor clue as to how to run a high-end security business. I went to work for him when I graduated college a year ago, and he has shown me a lot, but it is going to be really overwhelming, especially when I am not sure who to trust; which includes the family members sitting in my home right now."

"You think they might be involved?" He asked, surprised.

"Not really, but I do find it a little odd that they showed up this morning. I only remember seeing my aunt a couple of times in my entire life; she and Dad were not very close. The news reported him as being killed, and they show up at my front door."

"I somehow think you will handle them just fine, and if you need help, call. I will do everything I can." Knowing Steven Hoyt as well as he did, he could not imagine him having a sister that hated him enough to try to murder him. *But,* he thought, *just in case, I can run a background check.*

"Just find out what happened at our front door, and if my father is alive. I am going to get the bugs removed and find out who put them there. That is one thing I should be able manage pretty well, having a security business and all!"

"Are there any of your employees you can call on to help watch your back? Your dad usually hired some pretty good guys."

"I am not sure who just yet, not sure who to trust, or for that matter who is available. Dad kept everybody pretty busy and out on jobs."

He stopped and turned to her. "Do you trust me?"

She thought for a moment. "Yes, and I think Dad would have wanted me to."

"Then let me make a suggestion. I have a guy that just left the Navy; he was a SEAL too, like your dad. He's actually on his way here today, I was going to introduce him to your dad; see if he would hire him. I told your dad about him last week when we had lunch. He seemed to think he could use him. I think right now, maybe you could use him. I know he did quite a bit with

27

electronic surveillance; maybe he could help you there, or just watch your six.”

She was hesitant. What he said made sense, but she hesitated to ask someone to walk into what could be a life-threatening situation. “I don't know. . .”

“Just meet with him, see what you think.”

“Okay, but no promises.”

“I'll send him over tonight; his name is Kurt; Kurt Rutledge. Anything else you can think of that might help us? If the bugs turn up any information, please let me know.”

She shook her head. There were some things, but she was not ready to share with anyone just yet. She had to find out more on her own first, and before that she had to get some pushy relatives out of her house. "Not really, but we should talk soon."

He agreed and turned toward the road and his car while she went home.

Chapter Two

Sara walked into her house and almost immediately wanted to turn and run out again. Her aunt's overly shrill voice was loudly complaining about her keeping everyone waiting. *No wonder*

Dad never seemed to want her around, she thought.

"I'm here now, Aunt Ellie. What's the problem?"

"You kept this poor man waiting for nearly an hour . . ." Her aunt started.

"And, I am paying this, not-so-poor man, for his time, but," she turned to the man who had been sitting nearby when she walked in but was now standing, "I am sorry you had to listen to all this, Harry, when you said we needed to meet, I did not realize the police would be here and my aunt and uncle. My aunt seems to be under the impression you are here to read my father's will. Please correct that impression, and then we can go into my father's office and have our meeting."

Harry had been her father's attorney and legal adviser for as long as she could remember; she realized that she felt much closer to him than her own aunt and uncle.

"What on earth is she talking about, Mr. Reed? I thought you were here to read my brother's will."

Harry cleared his throat. "I'm afraid your niece is correct. Your brother has not been legally declared dead, as I understand it. The authorities do not have a body, only a rather large pool of blood out front that has not even been identified as your brother's."

"You said you were here to speak to my niece because of the attack on my brother. Why the hell are you here?"

"I am here to talk to her, not you, or your husband or your son, only Sara. I am sorry you had the wrong impression. I did not mean to mislead you."

Sara wanted to laugh; but thought better of it. "Aunt Ellie, there is a Hilton Hotel a couple of exits down the interstate. Please go there, give them this card," she handed her a business card, "tell them to bill the company. You can stay there for a few days, but I seriously think it would be better if you went home. It might be days or even weeks before we know anything, and I cannot have you staying here."

Her aunt sputtered. "You're throwing us out! What is wrong with you young lady? You don't even know what happened to your father, and we are your only relatives around. I can't . . . ."

"I am sorry," Sara interrupted her again, "I don't know what is going to happen over the next few days; or even weeks. I may have to travel, I will have to take care of our business, we don't really know anything. Please just go to the Hilton, or go home."

Harry stepped in, politely shuffling them toward the door. "Don't you worry, ma'am. We will make sure your niece will be fine. I have known your brother for many years, and I know he would expect me to make her a priority. Do you need a ride to the hotel or help with your luggage? Let's use the side door. You don't need to go through that scene out front."

Sara took a deep breath, and practically ran to the door of her Dad's home office. A quick code and then an eye scan, and she stepped into the dark office and flipped a switch on the wall. *There*, she thought, *that should block any electronic listening devices.*

Harry came back and found her with the lights on in her father's office, sitting at the small conference table. "I thought you might sit at the desk," he commented.

She shook her head. "I don't think I am big enough to fill that chair." she paused. "What am I going to do, Harry?"

"Now what would your dad say if he were here?   I know he would not expect you to be crying or down; he was a fighter and so are you. I've seen you in action. We don't know what happened or where he is, but I know he would want you to carry on, no matter what!"

She sighed. "I know, sorry, I just feel a little overwhelmed. All my fighting up to now has been play fighting, not real. This is real." She assumed he was talking about the karate matches she had competed in over the years. "What do we need to meet about?"

"A couple of weeks ago, your dad came in and had me write up a series of letters of instruction for you to give to the bank and some of your clients and employees, anyone who might question your authority."

"A couple of weeks ago. Why? What did he know?" she quickly asked.

He shook his head. "I don't know, hon. I thought it was a strange request, but he said it was a 'just in case' deal, he wasn't getting any younger, etc., etc."

"Something was going on. I don't know what, but he had an idea, Harry. He had an idea."

Harry stayed for a little over an hour, going over everything before leaving her alone. He asked repeatedly if she was going to be okay by herself and she assured him she would be fine. The doors would be locked, the security system activated, and she would be very careful to make sure she did not meet someone just outside any of her doors.

Chapter Three

It was nearly five in the afternoon when her doorbell rang. She had filled every minute after Harry left, putting all the training her father had drilled into her over the years to use, looking for any clues he might have left her. She was now convinced he had left the house alive; she was even pretty sure she knew how he left and that he had taken someone with him. Was that someone alive? That, she did not know.

She checked the pistol in her hand before responding to the door. "Who's there?"

"Kurt Rutledge, ma'am, Captain Jensen at the police department sent me."

She looked out the peephole; he was standing out away from the door where she could see him clearly. *He is not hard on the eyes,* she thought as she opened the door. "Come in, Mr. Rutledge."

"Mr. Rutledge is my father, ma'am. Please, just call me Kurt," He said as he picked up one end of a rolling load-out bag and rolled it through the door.

She put out her hand." Sara then, not ma'am."

He closed the door before shaking her hand. "It's a pleasure, ma---Sara." She smiled, and he felt his heart skip a beat. Wow, the captain had failed to mention how beautiful she was. She had changed from the shorts and tank top she was wearing earlier to jeans and a t-shirt, and Kurt decided she looked better in jeans than any girl he had ever met.

"Did Captain Jensen fill you in, 'cause this might not be all that much of a pleasure, Kurt. In fact, working with me right now could be really dangerous."

"He did, and I know your father by reputation ma'--- Sara. No matter how this turns out, I can't think of anyone I would rather help than you and your father."

They were still standing by the door. "Please, can I get you a coffee or iced tea? Come in, sit down, and you can tell me a little bit about yourself." She felt somewhat flustered by his presence. He was just too darn good-looking by far, and those eyes, those deep dark pools; she could hardly take her eyes off them or him.

"Thank you. I'd like to hear a little about what's going on from you, not third-hand. I understand you are pretty familiar with security and SEAL training."

She rolled her eyes. "I think my Dad started my training when I was about five, so yes, I have had a little introduction. He always wanted me to be able to defend myself—hand-to-hand combat, taekwondo, jujitsu, karate, marksmanship; with this."She showed him the .38 pistol still in her hand." Additionally, rifle training with a 30-30 all the way to an AK-47; to an AR-15 to a bow gun. Then of course we also did survival training in the woods." She paused to take a breath.

He held up his hands. "I give; I only hope I can keep up with you." He said with a grin, all the while thinking, she was incredible.

She smiled back, his smile lit up the room and made her heart skip a beat. She liked him, in spite of the fact she hadn't wanted to. She thought she would be better off alone, but now she found herself hoping he would stay and help her.

It was as though he were in tune with her thoughts. "I want to help, but I need to know what you know and what you think we should do. From there, I'll make suggestions and do what I can to help." He really did not want her to send him away. He felt drawn to her, and he wanted badly to have a chance to get to know her.

"I need to go back a few days; feel free to ask questions. I will try to fill you in on what I know and what I think or am guessing about." *Dear God, please don't let him think I'm crazy,* she thought.

"Fair enough." He nodded toward the couch. "Let's get comfortable." *Wow, that did not sound good,* he thought. Thankfully she did not seem to notice.

"I was in the airport in Frankfurt, Germany, the last time I talked with Dad. I tried to give him a quick synopsis of all my meetings, but he seemed distracted. Two things he said stand out from that conversation. The first was completely out of the blue and made no sense, 'Damn dragonflies; you got to watch out for them, honey.' The second was that he would get caught up when I got back, and, I quote, 'No matter what happens, I will always love you.' He never says things like that. He always says things like, 'Be safe, love ya, see ya soon.'"

"When I started to question him, he said he had to go and hung up. He was supposed pick me up at the airport, but when I landed he wasn't there. I waited for about half an hour, then I got an Uber and headed home. When I got to the corner up the street, there were cops, FBI, Secret Service, and I don't know who else, maybe NCIS, maybe others. They were everywhere; I don't know." She shook her head like it would clear out the memory, then took a deep breath and continued. "I got out and walked down the street to the barriers.

They let me through because I was family; some of them I am sure knew Dad personally. They told me a neighbor was out walking her dog and saw our front door was open and there was a large, very large, pool of blood on the front step. I remember hearing someone say they believed a pool that size probably meant the victim was more than likely deceased. One of the FBI agents wanted me to walk through the house and tell them if anything was missing."

She paused, and he urged her on. "Was there anything missing?"

She nodded, taking a moment. "Yes, but I didn't tell them. "When he started to protest, she added, "Come here; let me show you so you can understand." She wondered silently why she felt safer telling him than the authorities.

She walked to a door near the far end of the kitchen; it led to a staircase going down to the beach level. The door at the bottom opened out under the sundeck. Lined up against the wall were fishing gear, paddleboards, and scuba gear. "Here, does it look like anything is missing?"

He looked around. "No, but I don't know what's supposed to be here."

She turned and headed back up the stairs, once in the kitchen she continued. "Dad's paddleboard and scuba gear are gone. He moved everything so it wouldn't look like something was missing. Dad's office was locked, as usual. The officers wanted me to open it. We went in, and he had done the same thing. Where his go-bag was, things were shifted so it didn't appear anything was missing. He even fluffed the carpet when he rearranged things. That sort of cleanup takes time. I think he went to all that work because he knew I would be the only one noticing what was missing; he didn't want everyone to know. He knew I would notice, but I don't think he wanted anyone else to know, so I didn't tell them. He left plenty of tracks all over the beach; he knew the high tide would wipe out a single set of tracks into the water. I also believe that he put any sand that had blood on it, into the water; hence, he disappeared without a trace." She paused. "This has helped." He looked questioningly at her. "You know, I was mulling everything over and over.

Listing it all out has helped me put it into perspective."

"So you think he left via a paddleboard into the ocean. What about the attacker? There is a lot of blood out there, and you are right about that being a lot of work. Do you think all the blood is his? If so, how did he do it if he was bleeding badly?"

"The captain told me earlier that they know there is blood from two people on the step. I don't think he was hurt as bad as the other guy, I'm thinking it may be the attacker that's dead. I know it may be wishful thinking, but I just don't believe he's dead."

"Why didn't he just call the cops and get help?"

"That I don't know. I know he trusts Paul; maybe he is going after the ones responsible, or maybe he is trying to draw them away. I just don't know."

"Away from you or what, and how would he know there were others? It could have been a lone attacker."

"Again, I don't know. I just don't know." She was shaking her head again and was obviously upset. He wanted to take her in his arms and tell her everything would be okay, but he was pretty sure it would not be welcomed. She continued. "He knows me well enough to know I will ask questions and try to find answers, especially when I found these placed around the deck outside and near a couple of windows." She handed him a small but heavy box off the counter. "Lead-lined box, inside are listening devices. Whoever placed them must not have known Dad had sensors to let us know if a bug was in the area. He has a blocker we can turn on with the flip of switch, and by the way, it is on right now; I just hope it's working. When the authorities said I could come back here, I was already pretty sure I was being watched. Wait, I'm getting ahead of myself again. After going through the house with the FBI, they asked me to stay somewhere else for at least one night so their CSI techs could finish processing the scene. I did; last night, I went to a hotel down the road. I kept seeing a couple guys around everywhere I went, at dinner, in the lobby, at first I thought it might be FBI or the police or even the Secret Service watching me, but I don't know why they would watch me. Then my aunt called this morning. She, my uncle, and my cousin were here at the house and wanted to know where I was. I came home, but stopped by the police department on the way. No one said I couldn't come home, so I did."

"Your dad's sensors told you someone had bugged the place?" he asked.

"Yes, it sends a message to my and Dad's phones. What I don't understand why no one picked up on the bugs when they were here, but they didn't, or maybe they did and didn't share that information."

"Where is your dad's phone, do you know?"

"He left it; sitting on the kitchen counter."

"So what is the plan, or do you have one?" He asked quietly. So far he hadn't heard anything definitive that made him believe she was in all that much danger. Her dad really could have been the victim, and the perpetrator took his body and set everything up. In fact, knowing the FBI and the Secret Service, at the very least, were involved made him wonder if she could be over thinking everything. He knew either one of those agencies would have no problem bugging someone's home; and they would not be above making things look the way they wanted them to. He just knew he did not want to play her suspicions down and chase her away, but he didn't want to feed them either.

It was going to be a fine line he had to walk.

As if sensing his thoughts, Sara asked quietly. "You don't believe me, do you?"

"It's not that." He paused. "Really," He added when he saw her raised eyebrows. "It's just there are so many other what-if's, I would hate to think we focused on the wrong one." She started to protest. "Just hear me out, okay?"

"Okay." She nodded.

"I admit that there are several inconsistencies, and your conclusions could very well be true, but you have to admit that with the FBI and/or the Secret Service and/or the CIA involved with the investigation, there could be any number of explanations."

"I never said anything about the CIA; I don't think they're involved."

"I'm a SEAL, and I've heard a lot about your dad. Hell, he's considered legendary, so there are two things. First, I know your dad worked closely with them regarding some cartel in South America. It was way back when, but still he worked with them, and second, they are conspicuously missing from view right now. Your dad was a freaking congressman and a decorated hero. He did all sorts of missions overseas that the CIA was involved in, and they aren't here?" He shook his head. "I don't believe it."

She had to admit he might be right, but if he was, what then? Kurt noticed the dark circles under her eyes and her pale skin; she actually looked like she might collapse at any moment. "When did you eat last?"

"I don't know; yesterday dinner, I guess; I haven't really stopped today." She realized she really did feel famished.

"Let's go get something; there must be a few places to eat around here, and that will give us a chance to see if you're still being watched."

Chapter Four

Sara suggested a quiet restaurant not far away." Let me change into a pair of slacks, and we can head out; you will be fine like you are." She answered his questioning look before he actually asked. "It's pretty casual out here at the beach. Some people show up in shorts and swim tops; I just never have."

They arrived at the restaurant a short time later. Kurt thought it looked fancy to him, but he noticed she had been correct about the patrons; everything from shorts and tank tops to suits and ties. The tables were set up to give the diners considerable privacy. Many of the tables were next to windows that overlooked the ocean; it was at one of these tables that they were seated.

The owner knew Sara and her father quite well, as they often came here to eat, and he came out to their table to express his condolences. "I am so, so sorry to hear about your father, my dear. He was a wonderful, wonderful man."

"We don't know anything for sure, Mr. Rantolli, it's only speculation in the news right now; the police do not know anything for sure."

"Oh my, what wonderful news. Your dear father may be alive and well. We need to celebrate; let me bring your favorite dish, my dear."

Sara looked to Kurt for some help."We just don't know, sir. I just wanted Sara to have a good quiet meal, to try to get away from all the hubbub, if you know what I mean."

"Of course, of course. We will keep everything a quiet as possible; you don't need to worry about a thing. Your dinner with be here very soon. You two can have this room all to yourselves."

"Wow," was all Kurt could say when he walked away.

She smiled ruefully, and began tapping on the table with her spoon, not hard but enough to create some noise. "The news put out early on that Dad had been killed, and not one of them has retracted the statement, so everyone thinks he's dead! On another note, though, I think I know what he was talking about when he said to 'watch out for the dragonflies'."

"What?" He asked quickly, looking around.

She kept tapping. "Look out the window at the handrail. There is a dragonfly on it, but it's not real. It's a drone, and it is probably trying to record what we are talking about. Dragonflies hide at night and avoid where there are a lot of birds. They are prey for birds, and I don't see a single seagull paying this one any mind."

"Maybe we should move over there?" He gestured to a table against the inside wall as far from the window as one could get.

"Good idea." She quickly swooped up her purse and drink and headed for the suggested table. Her mind was quickly clicking off ideas. *What would they want with her? She didn't know where her father was; she couldn't lead them to him. On the other hand, what if they were planning on taking her to get him to come to them?*

"I think I need to go to the office. I think, what we need will be there, and then we can maybe go camping."

"Wait, why? And where?"

She looked him in the eye and thought for a moment. Did she trust him enough to take him with her? He stared back, not blinking, as if he knew exactly what her thoughts were. "If I tell you, then you are in. I don't know for how long or where or how dangerous it's going to get, but I am more convinced than ever that whoever is watching me is either waiting for a chance to grab me and get Dad to come to save me, or they are waiting for him to contact me, or me him. I need to get away so I can find him or him me."

"I'm in," he responded. He knew right then she had not shared all her thoughts or knowledge of what was going on. There was no hesitation. He knew he would give it all to help her or save her, whatever it took.

"Are you carrying?" She asked.

"No, had to turn in all my weapons when I checked out."

He was not sure what she was doing when she bent over until a few moments later when she came up with an ankle holster, holding a small handgun." Take this for now. When we get back to the office, we can get you setup."

"Okay." He slid it off the table and quickly bent over, put it on, and pulled his pant leg over it. "Little tight, but it will do for now." He noted silently that she handled guns like it was second nature.

Their dinner arrived a few moments later, and they ate mostly in silence. Finally feeling full at last, Sara sat back. "We can head over to the office now. I don't care if we're followed for now; in fact, I would like to draw them out a bit to see if we can get a handle on who they are. I would love to get my hands on that drone. It might hold some answers."

From the restaurant they went directly to her dad's business, a nondescript warehouse in the industrial district downtown. She pulled her car up to the guard shack. "Billy did you draw the night shift again?"

"Ms. Sara, what are you doing here? Is there any word on your daddy yet?"

"Afraid not. Billy, this is Kurt. He was a new hire of Dad's, and I sort of hijacked him to help me until we know what's going on. Kurt, Billy. He works the guard gate, usually in the daytime. Where's Jason?"

Billy shook his head. "Don't really know, he never showed for his shift. I told Rick I would work until Jason showed or he found someone else to relieve me."

Sara felt a wave of nausea. This was not good. Jason was relatively new. Billy was good, but he was older and might be easier to take down if someone planned a direct attack.

"Maybe I should wait out here?" Kurt suggested, again as if in tune with her thoughts.

"No, I think we should shut the gate and put up the bollards. Billy should come inside, and we need to find out what happened to Jason. Shut the gate behind me, Billy, and raise the bollards. At least anyone coming at us with a vehicle will get slowed down."

Billy immediately turned into the guard shack to do her bidding as she pulled forward; he never questioned her authority or the why. He quickly closed the gate and hit a button that raised bollard poles strong enough to stop anything short of a tank, then walked to the back door of her car and jumped in.

Sara opened an app on her phone, and one of the large warehouse doors opened, and then shut immediately after she drove through. "Kill the Wi-Fi, Billy, and turn on the jammers. We need to figure out what's going on."

"You think this has something to do with your daddy?"

"I do. What's Dad always saying? 'I don't believe in coincidences, I do, however, believe in conspiracies.'"

Billy laughed heartily as he went to do her bidding. "Those beliefs saved him many a time!"

"So what now?" Kurt asked, as he wondered if she really needed his help. She seemed almost crazily capable, but he so wanted to stay with her and help.

She seemed calm and matter-of-fact, like she was doing nothing more out of the ordinary than ordering a mocha frappuccino at Starbucks, but on the inside her mind was racing and her stomach was doing flip-flops. She was sure she would do something wrong and fail her father. "Now I need to make a couple of phone calls and probably change some access codes. I don't know if this place has been compromised or not, but I don't want to take any chances. Have Billy open up the armory room so you can get armed. I will be right back."

What is here that someone would want? She asked herself over and over as she made her way to the offices.

It was several minutes before she came back out. Now dressed in dark battle fatigues, looking more soldier than Kurt thought possible, but still beautiful. He noted to himself that he had never seen fatigues look so good on anyone before.

She interrupted his thoughts. "I called Jason. No answer, so I called Captain Jensen at the MPD to see if they can find him." She turned to Billy. "I sent a message out to all the employees, including Rick, telling them to be extra vigilant and to only message me, no one else, if they needed something. I also said I would be shuttering the office for at least a week. They will be paid as usual, but there will not be anyone here to handle any requests."

"Won't that essentially shut the business down?" Kurt asked.

"Maybe, maybe not. Most of our employees work for very wealthy people as bodyguards or at special events.

Nearly all are retired Special Forces from one branch or another of the service, and they are all well trained and very capable and resourceful. I think they can handle it, and if they can't, they can call me. Maybe it will tell us what all this is about."

"Good idea." Billy cheered her on. "What do you want me to do?"

"This one is a lot to ask, but how would you feel about staying here? The place is fully stocked with food, and there is a bed and a shower and satellite TV. I want to know if anyone attempts to get in here. No one should, especially our employees. I told them the office was closed; do not come in, so literally not one person has a reason to be here, except us."

"And where are you going to be, just in case I need you?"Billy asked.

She handed him a phone. "Here's a sat phone; it's encrypted. You can use it to call me without worrying, and I have this one." She added, "and, if Dad is alive, he will try to reach us this way when he finds the cells off. Extra battery packs are in the armory on the chargers. We are going to get some camping gear and go camping."

Billy looked surprised but didn't ask. He had known her and her father long enough to know that they played strategy games just for fun; and he often said that Steve and Sara were masters at strategic maneuvers. Sara had a plan; he was just happy he could help her.

It was past midnight when they finished loading a matte-black Toyota

4x4 pickup with two dirt bikes, basic clothes, tents, food, a variety of weapons, and for safety's sake a well stocked first aid kit. Sara went over each item carefully before she felt that everything was ready. "Let's take a short nap, and then we'll head out."

Kurt agreed quickly; he was beginning to think she was like the energizer bunny and didn't stop for anything. He knew she had been on the go for at least twenty-four hours, as had he.

Chapter Five

Dawn was breaking when they headed out. Billy was settled in, there was still no word on Jason and no word from her father, and she was having a hard time holding out hope. Her eyes burned with unshed tears almost constantly.

"I am guessing you have a plan of sorts?" Kurt asked when they were on the road.

"Yeah, I guess, sort of. I am hoping to draw them out. If we are away from help and appear vulnerable, then maybe we can find out what they're after."

"That's why you don't care if they follow us. Any ideas on what we do if we are outnumbered or outgunned?"

She smiled. "Sorry you came?" She hoped he was not going to back out now; his presence was helping her remain calm.

"No, no, just making sure you thought this through." He was more than a little impressed with her training and expertise. He had served with a lot of guys that didn't think as strategically as she seemed to, but at the same time, they did not know who or what they were up against.

"If we believe we are outgunned or outnumbered, then we will do our

71

level best to lose them. Where we are heading, Dad and I have been to several times a year for years now. I should know the area well enough to be able to lose them tracking us if we need to. I have only seen guys in suits. Are they going to be prepared for Dad's survival classroom? What'd ya think?"

"I think you are one of the smartest women I have ever met. It is an honor, ma'am." He thought for a moment of how he would feel if she were in imminent danger right in front of him. He tamped the thought down, realizing it would be the worst feeling he could think of.

That day they took the truck as far as they could into the High Sierras east of Sacramento. Sara stopped at a small area that he agreed would be easily defensible. Backed by rock, they had a good view of the road leading in. Any other direction in would require the navigation of treacherous territory. There was a small cave in the rocks behind; Sara suggested they sleep in it. "I saw you pack a trip line; I'll set it up," he said. "That way we can both get some sleep and be rested for tomorrow."

"Good idea. I'll get some dinner going." *It seems too easy,* she thought, *I can work with him, and we each do what is needed with hardly a thought, just like Dad and I, only we barely know each other. It isn't just the SEAL training; he seems in tune with me.* That thought made her feel both excited and scared at the same time. There was a funny feeling in the pit of her stomach that she didn't recognize. "Tomorrow we'll take the bikes; after that it's going to get tougher.   I haven't seen any drones for a while, have you?"

"No, but I don't think that necessarily means we lost them."

After a quiet meal, they put out their sleeping bags and settled in for the night, side arms at the ready so they could sleep easy.

They lay quietly on opposite sides of a small fire for warmth. Each was engrossed in their own thoughts; Sara could not remember being so drawn to anyone in her life. She had often met guys she thought attractive, but Kurt was in a league all his own. She found herself longing to be lying much closer to him. Kurt, on the other hand, felt like it was all he could do to keep from drawing her nearer. He wanted her like no one else he had ever met, and that made sleep elusive for each of them for a while.

Sara woke with a start, Kurt's hand over her mouth. He signaled her to be quiet and listen. It was a good distance off, but she could hear them, dirt bikes? She wasn't sure, but that's what it sounded like. "Come on," she whispered, quietly slipping out of the cave to check the road leading to where they had stopped.

There were several lights bobbing several miles away, and they were not trying to hide. She shook her head. "If we're lucky we have an hour. Considering how many there are, I don't think we want a showdown. If we take the bikes they will be able to follow us easily. Are you up for a hike?" She asked.

He nodded. "Let's put the bikes and extra supplies in the cave. They may think we left on them and not see them in the cave, and that will give us an advantage." She agreed and thirty minutes later, backpacks on, he followed her out of camp into the darkness.

By dawn they could no longer hear the bikes, so they decided to take a short break, under an outcropping of rocks behind some brush. They had hardly spoken since leaving the camp. She broke the silence, "Thank you, that was close. I'm sorry I was sleeping so sound."

"Are you kidding? I finally felt useful." He smiled at her. "That's what you brought me along for. I was happy to be of service."

His smile made her feel more lighthearted than she should have under the circumstances. She pulled out a pair of binoculars from her backpack." Are those M22's?" He asked.

"Yes, they are. Want to try them and see if our friends are on foot or if we lost them?"

"'Sure." He took them from her outstretched hand. "I hope we lost 'em, but I am not holding my breath."

She waited quietly while he studied their back trail. "Couple of miles; they are down by the stream we crossed a while back. These guys are good, really good. I am guessing some of them are Special Forces. It's not going to be easy to lose them, right now they are circling, trying to find a clue as to which direction we took."

She pointed to a ridge on the other side of a steep ravine. "That is where we're going; there is a cabin up there. If Dad is up here, I think that's where he'll be, but we have to lose them before we head there. All things considered and how many seem to be after us, I think I would rather find my dad than find out who these guys are."

He was glad she finally trusted him enough to tell him where they were heading. "You know those big pines we passed, right down there?" He pointed to a spot about five hundred yards down the hill." I think, if we can get to them and get up into the trees, we can take cover in the branches and let them go past us. Once we are clear we can head over to the ridge and the cabin. If we keep going up and over it might be easier terrain, but we are going to be above the tree line pretty soon, and then we won't have any cover."

She agreed, and they spent a few minutes leaving a misleading trail before heading back down to the trees Kurt had pointed out. They wrapped their shoes with heavy socks from their backpacks and moved carefully so as to not leave any tracks to follow or give their location away.

Chapter Six

Sara woke with a start, but she did not move. Kurt was in a nearby tree; she hoped he heard them coming. It seemed like hours since they had climbed the trees and laid themselves out on the thick branches. Her face hurt where the rough bark cut into it, but they were so close she dared not move. She could hear them softly talking, but it was only when they were almost underneath her that she could make out what they were saying.

"What the hell are we doing out here, man? I did not sign up for chasing some American chick through hell and back so some South American asshole can torture her to find out where her papa is. I say we need to get out of here." The larger of the two was speaking.

"Would you shut up? The last guy that tried to leave got gut-shot. I would rather chase the girl than get gut-shot. Besides, we don't know what he'll do to her," the other responded.

"Dude, I'm not stupid and neither are you. You know what Salazar is capable of. I say we cut out now, head down the ridge over to our right, and get while the getting is good. We don't go back to camp, and we get down the hill and disappear, even if we have to change our names. I don't want anything to do with these guys, especially Salazar. The man's a f'ing psycho."

"You think we can do it? You think we can get away clean and not have him chase us down for sport?" The smaller one sounded hopeful.

"Look, if we just disappear, don't go back to camp, just disappear, I think we can get away. He is not going to want to waste time on us. He wants her; to him she's more important than us."

Sara could no longer hear them as they kept moving. Her thoughts were racing. Was this a ruse to get them out of hiding? Who was Salazar, and why did he want her dad? She shifted quietly, just enough to get the bark that was stabbing her face moved to a new position. They needed to wait, twenty minutes, maybe longer; until they were sure the coast was clear, before they moved positions.

Time dragged by slowly. Twenty minutes got extended, time and again, as more of Salazar's men crossed beneath their hiding place, all heading up the hill. Sara realized they had been in the trees the better part of the day. Soon it would be dark again. None of them seemed to have any idea how close they were to their prey; most seemed to be speaking Spanish. Sara and Kurt waited. *How long have we been up here*, she wondered. The groups that had headed up the hill were now coming back down. She didn't understand a lot of Spanish, but it was enough for her to understand they were going back to the main camp; they would start out in the morning trying to pick up her trail again.

Kurt jumped down from his tree and signaled her to do the same. "Did you hear what they said about Salazar and why they are after me?" She whispered.

"Only part of it. Who the hell is Salazar?"

"I don't know, but I think I know who can help us find out. We just have to figure out how to get back down off this mountain."

"Not yet, it's not time," another voice whispered from the side.

"Daddy? Daddy, are you all right? Is that really you?"

"Hush, follow me, I'll explain later." Her father moved silently away with only a brief nod in Kurt's direction.

She fell in a few steps behind her father and Kurt a few behind her. A thousand questions revolved around her mind like a race car on a round track, but she knew when he said 'hush' he meant it. It seemed like they walked for hours. They moved silently down into a ravine and, crossed a creek, jumping from one rock to another so as to not get their boots wet, and then climbed back up the other side. Sara's legs ached; they were tired and sore already, and her father was setting a blistering pace on the climb out of the ravine. The sun had been setting when they started, and she was sure it was close to dawn when her father paused. He signaled her and

Kurt to precede him between two large rocks. It was a tight squeeze, but Sara kept moving along between what appeared to be the rocky side of the mountain and large boulders, Kurt followed, sometimes having to beat down the panic he felt when she would momentarily disappear.

Finally they stepped out into what appeared to be a large hollow in the side of the mountain at the mouth of a cave. Even though their eyes were adjusted to the darkness, it was so dark Sara hesitated to move forward; not knowing what was in front of her. Her father walked past her and started a camp lantern, flooding the dark with light. A pool of water was off to the side, apparently filled by a mountain spring; a bedroll with what appeared to be a stash of food was against the back wall.

"We can talk here; I don't think our voices will carry outside of this area."

"Wherever here is," Sara commented dryly as she noticed a dark red stain on her dad's shirt. "Daddy, you're bleeding," she stated, her voice not changing pitch.

He looked down, "Damn it, I must have busted the stitches open." He turned to Kurt. "I don't know who you are, or why you are with my daughter, but you seem pretty savvy. Can you check over there where we came in and see if I dripped any blood? If I did, they will be on us today."

"Yes sir; Kurt Rutledge, sir," he quickly added while he turned to do Steven Hoyt's bidding.

Kurt pulled a small flashlight from his backpack. It was so dim that the light did not carry far, and he went to check their path. Meanwhile, Sara pulled out a small first aid kit. "How bad is it, and are you going to explain what the hell is going on, Dad?"

"It goes back a ways, way back, like back when I met your mom. "He paused, and Sara looked surprised. "Salazar's daddy was a well-known mechanic known as *'El Lobo'*; he was the one who shot your mom."

"But he was killed getting away, wasn't he?" she asked, while pulling his shirt up to reveal a blood-soaked bandage.

"Yes, he was. Salazar was a young man, newly married with a newborn at the time. The whole Salazar family has always been involved with the drug trade, running coyotes up from South America and any number of other illegal activities. Salazar raised his son to follow in the family's business dealings, only the son got careless. He likes to be a playboy, and he got caught. He is sitting in federal lockup awaiting trial, and Daddy is not happy."

Sara was carefully removing the bandage when Kurt came back and gave a quick shake of his head, indicating he found no blood. "So what has all this have to do with you and Mom? That was years ago."

"A couple of things. One, Salazar has always blamed me for his papa's demise." He held up his hand when Sara started to protest. "Secondarily, and probably the thing that has brought all this to a head is that we, meaning Hoyt Securities, are guarding the main guy that turned state's evidence against his boy."

"Excuse me?" When did that happen and why? I would've thought that to be the marshal's' or FBI's jurisdiction. How did you get involved?" She sounded less than pleased as she pulled off the last of the tape holding the bandage, causing her father to wince in pain.

"I was getting to that, if you will let me finish? It was a joint effort that got the young Salazar caught, DEA, FBI, Homeland, and the CIA, and us, Hoyt Security, all of us working together made it happen, but the CI that gave them the info was a guy who worked on a couple of jobs for me a few years ago. He agreed to testify if I was in charge of keeping him safe until the trial. In fact, he said he would refuse to cooperate unless I was in charge of his safety."

"So we have him, somewhere safe, and Salazar sent someone to get you, so you would tell them where the informant was."

"See how quick she picked up on that, Kurt?"

"Yes sir. Your daughter is very quick and very smart, sir." Kurt was still standing off to the side.

Sara looked at each one like she would like to hit them. "Kurt, I think we need to clean this up and superglue the wound shut and then re-bandage it; it looks pretty deep. I just hope you are not bleeding internally." She pointed to the first-aid kit. "Everything we need should be in there. So what happened at our front door?"

"I was getting to that." Steve grimaced as she started cleaning the wound. "One guy, he, caught me off guard. I am not sure how he got to the front door without my knowing, but he did. We fought, I truly believe he was instructed to bring me in alive, so they could torture me to get Adolfo's whereabouts, which gave me the advantage, as I did not need to be that cautious. I managed to kill him and with Rick's help got rid of the body for a couple of days. The police probably have it by now."

"So Rick knows what is going on? He never said a word to me, didn't even call me when I got back. I never even heard from him. Billy did. He had Billy stay because Jason never showed for his shift. I shut the office down. Billy is staying inside, and we put the place on lockdown. I wasn't sure who to trust."

"So you took a stranger in?" Steve indicated Kurt.

"Not exactly. He's the candidate you were supposed to meet with, the one Paul told you about. I was going to come alone, but I decided I could trust him, and so far he has not let me down."

"I remember Paul telling me about you. It was last week; seems about a lifetime ago." Steve extended his hand."

"I am honored to help, sir." Kurt shook his hand. "You said we couldn't go down the hill yet, so are we going to sit it out up here, sir? It looks like you have been here a while. Is there a good place to keep an eye out from? I can take the first watch."

"Appreciate the offer. I have the perimeter set up with some sensors. There's a cave entrance over in the corner that's pretty defensible, if they get as far as here. In a pinch we could get out the back way from the cave, and I happen to have a pretty decent stockpile of ammo back there. I've used this place as training camp a few times over the years."

"I remember now, you brought me here when I was about eight or nine. That's when you found it, right? It was on the way up to the cabin. I actually thought that's where you would be."

"That's right, I've come up here a few times with new guys when I wanted to see how qualified they were in their strategic training. I rigged the cabin. It was too obvious a hideout; anyone who breaks in up there will be unpleasantly surprised.

Having finished cleaning the wound, Sara placed a generous amount of superglue on it, and held it closed. Steve winced again; the glue stung fiercely. "I'm beginning to think she's enjoying herself," he said to Kurt while grimacing.

She smiled. "You still have a lot of splaining to do! I intend to get the full story before this is over. I assume we are waiting for the trial to start and then we will head down."

"Actually, we are waiting for some reinforcements. Salazar never comes up here to the States, but he is here now and we intend to get him. He is the 'Big Fish' in all this. I was not intending you get involved with this part." He smiled at her, "I should have known better though. But honey, this could get real messy, Salazar is not going to come quietly; he is going to try to take out as many of us as he can."He held up his hand as she started to protest, "I know, I have taught you to fight and to shoot, but this will be different. This is for real."

"I get it, Dad. I laid in that tree yesterday and wondered how long it would be before they figured out where we were.   I held my breath until I thought I was going to turn purple and pass out, and I have never been so scared in my whole life.   I will do whatever I can to help, just don't send me away.   Let me stay with you and help, please."

"I've got her six, sir; I will do whatever is needed to help." Kurt spoke up and, she smiled at him. He thought to himself. *Her smile could light up my world. Please, God, give me a steady hand and heart to keep her safe."* He prayed quietly.

"Then we wait, you didn't happen to bring anything good to eat, did you? MRE's have never been my favorite, and that's all I've had for the last few days."

"You wish," was her laughing response.

Chapter Seven

They all settled in for what could be a long wait. Kurt took the opportunity to try to get to know Sara better.

"Tell me about yourself. All I know so far is that you know more about being a SEAL than any civilian I've met."

She smiled. "You know, most people think it was Dad's idea and that he wanted me to be a SEAL, but it was never that, was it, Dad?"

"No, baby, it was never that. I just wanted you to be able to take care of yourself."

"Daddy, you said that Salazar blamed you for his papa's death. I don't understand why. I thought the guy died when he tried to kill Mom. Didn't he run away and get hit by a car?"

"I'm not sure why the family twisted the story. Actually, he was killed when your Mom's dog chased him out into traffic."

"Now that sounds like a story." Kurt encouraged him to continue. "What happened? I'd like to hear, if you don't mind."

"Her mom saw an agent get run down by a hit-and-run driver; she didn't know he was an agent at the time. She went to help him. He was carrying a message for me, and he gave it to her and told her with his dying words to give it to me and no one else. That was how we met. The people that took out the agent were none too happy about her giving it to me. Things were a big mess.

Took us several weeks to figure out the code it was written in, and actually decipher the message. Her mom was a target until then. She had a photographic memory, so we thought they would try to kidnap her, and torture her, not try to kill her."

"Mom had a photographic memory? I didn't know that!"

"She always said it was no big deal, it was just a good memory, but it was she who figured out the message. That was when the people behind the whole problem hired Salazar's papa, he was known as El Lobo, to take your mom out. We don't know what went wrong, or right, in my opinion. Your mom was riding when he shot at her. We don't know if he just missed or your mom's horse spooked or what. We heard shots, and we all went running, I will never forget seeing your mom lying over her horse's neck, blood everywhere." His voice faltered with the memory. "I couldn't get her hands free. They were tangled in his mane, and there was so much blood my hands kept slipping." He shook his head. "I have never been so scared in my whole life, until now. One thing you both need to know; whatever happens tomorrow, do not let these people take any of us alive. They do unspeakable things to their enemies. If push comes to shove, take your own life, don't get taken," he added quietly. "I mean it. Death is way better than what they are capable of."

Sara and Kurt nodded, both more than a little shocked by his statement. What could they say in response to that?

"Where is your Mom, if you don't mind my asking?" Kurt inquired, trying to change the subject.

"She died in a accident when I was almost five," Sara responded quietly.

"I am so sorry."

"That reminds me." Sara turned to her father. "Aunt Ellie showed up with Uncle Jerry and Clive. She was under the mistaken impression that you had died, so she decided to show up and try to take over, kinda like she did at Mom's funeral."

"You remember that?" Steve asked.

"I remember her voice. It's so shrill. I remember her telling me that I needed to dress properly for a girl. I had changed into jeans after the funeral and gone to the barn to see the horses. And then I remember that she turned to you and said something to the effect of you having no business raising a daughter; that she would take me with her so I could grow up with a proper upbringing. I think I was petrified. I don't remember what else she said, though, because you picked me up and held me close and told me, "'It's you and me. No one is taking you anywhere. You are my daughter!'"

Steve smiled. "I think she has said something like that nearly every time she has seen you since. She called me one time when your picture was in the newspaper and you were dressed in fatigues at a base somewhere. A news photographer had snapped a picture of you shooting an AR-15 at the range.”

“Well, if my opinion counts at all, sir, I think you did a hell of a job. She’s smart, she has more savvy than most on figuring out strategies, and if you don’t mind my saying, I think she looks great in fatigues.” Kurt injected.

Steve noticed Sara looking at Kurt.” Thank you, Kurt. That means a lot,” she managed, feeling more than a little tongue-tied.

“And I think it’s time we turned in,” Steve stated calmly. “Kurt, you have first watch.   Even with the sensors I think we should use extra caution. Call me in two hours. Sara, you get some rest. I’ll wake you in four.”

It was a long while before Sara slept, and then it was not very restful; her father's words kept chasing through her mind. She thought about her father and Kurt. They had both seen dead bodies and been in plenty of real life-and-death situations. Her father had given her the training, but this would be very different and she knew it. *Dear God, it's in your hands. Please protect us, in Jesus' name,* she prayed silently before falling asleep.

Kurt found a good spot to watch their back trail while his mind was busy going over all that had happened over the last few days. He reluctantly acknowledged to himself that he was rapidly falling for Sara; she was the first girl he had ever met that he could carry on a conversation with. He felt in sync with her.   He prayed that when this whole thing was over, they would have the opportunity to see where their relationship could go.

Steve did not fall asleep right away either.   He had noticed the way Sara and Kurt looked at each other.   He remembered how Sandi had made him feel the first time he laid eyes on her. His biggest concern now was getting them through the next few days in one piece.

Chapter Eight

The satellite phone clicked a short while later. Her father answered it; Kurt came in from where he had been on watch. The message was short. "There are about twenty men headed toward you, about two clicks out. They have a dog. Reinforcements are about a half click behind that and closing, also help from helo is incoming. Stay safe, head on a swivel."

"They aren't in sight yet, sir," Kurt put in.

Steve turned to Sara and Kurt. "They will be soon. They're close and they have a dog, so they will find us. Help is right behind, but before help arrives it is going to get ugly."

"Daddy, I would hate to shoot a dog; it's not its fault. Is there anything we can do?"

Kurt's heart went out to Sara. She was not prepared for what was about to happen. He wanted to do whatever he could to make it easier for her. "We could try to snare it, sir, when it comes through the opening there. Course what we do when it's caught or if we miss . . ." Kurt let their imaginations finish the sentence.

"Daddy?" Sara looked for him to do what he had always done, fix it, protect her, and fix it.

Steve sighed. "Kurt, fix a snare, but you two have to be prepared to shoot to kill it and anyone else that comes through that opening. You too, Sara, do not hesitate. If Kurt misses you will have no choice but to shoot to kill. If you catch him, Kurt, I'll tackle him and choke him down, and then tie him up. We will deal with how to handle him later; hopefully, we can stop him from ripping one or all of us to shreds." He shook his head as if in disbelief that he let his daughter talk him into even trying. "Sara, you will probably have to take down his handler. We've got to hurry; we have maybe ten minutes."

Sara mouthed the words *thank you* to her father before volunteering to help Kurt. Eight minutes later they were ready, each person in their place, weapons ready. Each held their breath, as they controlled their own thoughts; Kurt was trying hard not to think of what he would do if Sara got hurt or worse. Steve wondered if he would have the strength to tackle and hold the dog. He had to; he could not watch it attack his daughter. He prayed she would have the strength of mind to do what was necessary. Of Kurt, he knew he was already battle tested; *just give him a sure hand and eye, Lord.*

The dog burst through the small space; he was caught. Steve jumped on him. Shots were fired; one man fell next to where Steve lay on the dog. More shots were fired outside their small area; it sounded like a full-on firefight. To Sara it seemed like an eternity before it quieted down.

"Steven Hoyt, sir?"

"Here."

"Clear, sir. Salazar is not here, sir." A soldier stepped through the opening. "Fourteen in custody; four deceased; make that fifteen in custody." He paused when the dog handler moaned. "Need a medic in here." He then stepped around the dog handler, lying where he had fallen. He seemed surprised to see Sara and Kurt.

"Damn it, how'd he get away?" Steve demanded.

"Not sure, sir. We have a small party trying to pick up his trail, sir. I did not realize you had your daughter with you, sir."

"She got here last night. I need you to keep her safe and get her down off this mountain. Kurt, are you with me?"

"Yes sir!"

"Good, then let's go." He turned to Sara. "I see an argument coming. Don't; just go home, and stay inside until this is over. These guys will get you there. I don't want to have to worry about you. Let's go, Kurt." He added over his shoulder. "Beside's, that dog is going to need some attention. You wanted us to save him."

Sara stood without speaking for a few moments. It had all taken a turn so quickly, from wondering if they would live a few moments earlier to the hunted becoming the hunters. She mulled over her father's words about the dog. He was right; she had wanted him to save him, but that was as far as her thoughts had gone. Not what was she going to do with him. Her father made one thing pretty clear; the dog was now her responsibility, and one never shirked a responsibility.

She tried to analyze her emotions. She realized that for the first time in her life she had shot someone, not a target, but a real person, a person that had every intention of siccing his dog on them and possibly killing or maiming one or more of them. She looked at him as a medic worked over him, and realized that all she felt was relief that he was down and they were all okay.

Chapter Nine

Sara watched in silence as her father, Kurt, and half a dozen men disappeared through the rocks. She turned to the man left in charge of her safety, not sure what would happen next. She asked him as politely as she could, "What's next?" She realized that while she was happy they had all survived the last few minutes, she was pretty angry at being sent away.

"There are four helos on the way in, ma'am, one for the wounded and medics, one for the dead, one for us, and one for the prisoners. Anyone left will hoof it down to the Humvees and drive out."

"You are all National Guard, aren't you?"

"No, ma'am; some of us are DEA; most are a lesser-known Homeland squad. This group is kind of special. Most of us have been handpicked for this type of op, ma'am."

"Please call me Sara. What kind of op is this?" She was starting to calm down.

"I think it might be best for me not to explain further. Just know that your safety is our priority." He indicated a circle of three other men all standing near her.

"I am going to check on the dog and sit with him while we wait." She walked over and sat on the ground next to the dog that was tied and bound. Even though he was lying still, he seemed to be struggling to breathe. Sara reached for the straps around his muzzle.

"That is no puppy, ma'am. He is a dangerous animal that can rip your face off."

"What's your name, soldier?"

"Most folks call me Hondo. Not my given name, but they all call me that."

"Well, Hondo, I didn't risk my life to help save this dog from being shot so we could suffocate him. Somehow I have to make sure he can breathe and hopefully convince him that I mean him no harm." With that she turned back to the dog and loosened the straps around his muzzle; not removing, just loosening. Calmly talking to him and stroking his side, she waited while he relaxed more. His collar was woven with *ZEUS* in bold capital letters repeating itself around his neck. He seemed in good health. "What do you think, Hondo, Spanish, German, or English commands?"

He was impressed with her ability to calm the animal so quickly, but he was leery. He had seen Malinois in action; they were fast and strong and could easily take down a couple hundred pound grown man. "I don't know, ma'am, but you could try each one to see what works."

Sara made sure she had a good hold on his makeshift leash and began loosening the straps around his legs. "Zeus, stay." She used a commanding voice, hoping he would understand the command. Zeus lay quietly, not moving other than turning his head to look at her. He did not growl; he just watched her.

Zeus felt no fear of this young woman. She had a soft touch and did not seem to be an enemy. He liked the feel of her hands as she ran them through his fur.

Sara stood up slowly and backed away a few feet, not wanting to startle Zeus and get a bad reaction. "Zeus, come," she commanded in English, hoping he knew that command as well.

Zeus jumped to his feet and trotted to her side and sat down. "Wow, how cool is that?" she asked Hondo.

"Pretty cool, but don't forget what this dog is trained for. Give me a minute; I will ask the guys if they have worked with service dogs like him."

She watched him walk over to his men and talk with them, and then Sara took the leash and walked around the camp with Zeus. For his part, Zeus didn't really understand all that was happening. He did understand that this young woman reminded him of his first mistress. She had been kind and good to him, and he had not protected her, and she had quit moving one day. As she lay on the ground bleeding, he had been taken away and had never seen her again. Zeus determined right then he would not let that happen again.

Hondo started back toward them with another soldier. Zeus growled; no one was going to take him away again. "Zeus, no, sit!" Sara commanded, hoping the words would control him. He sat, but there was still a low growl in his throat.

"I think he's decided you are his new human." The soldier spoke in a quiet, calm voice. "He's been through a lot in the last few minutes; it's pretty impressive that you have gotten this far with him. Just take it very slow. I'm Jake; I worked with a soldier in Afghanistan that had a bomb-sniffing dog. They are impressive animals; just keep in mind how strong he is."

Sara nodded. "Not a problem. I just hope we can get him down the hill and figure out his commands. So far he seems to be responding to English commands; I'm pretty sure he has had some pretty extensive training." Zeus had stopped growling, so long as no one came too close to Sara.

"He is probably picking up on your body signals as well. Malinois are really smart," *and really dangerous*, he added silently. "I think I hear the helos coming in. We will be out of here shortly."

Zeus heard the helicopters too and did not seem too happy about them. He had been taken away from his first mistress in one, he was forced into one to come here, and he did not like them. He started to back away, but when Sara did not move he had to save her. He got in front of her and pushed back against her. He tried and tried to get her to move away from those huge noisy machines, but Sara did not move so Zeus sat between her and the machines, growling and trembling at the same time.

Sara was not immune to Zeus's actions; it was pretty obvious it was going to be a project to get him in a helo. One of Hondo's men came up with a helmet and a tactical vest, "You need to put this on, ma'am, and we need to get ready for the next bird."

Zeus stood up and growled; no one was going to get near his human. "Zeus, it's okay. Sit. Stay." He sat, but he still growled. "Toss it." She held out her hand to catch first the vest and then the helmet. *This is going to get real interesting,* she thought.

She looked over at Hondo. "What do you think about us 'hoofing it' down to the Humvees?"

"Why? The helos are the fastest way to get you out of here."

Sara decided to take the blame rather than Zeus. "I really hate to fly, and honestly I would rather walk than fly, please."

Hondo was already wondering if they were going to have a problem getting the dog on board; maybe this would be the best solution. She would have more soldiers protecting her, as the Humvees would have more guys. "Okay, it'll take a little longer but let's do that. You take the dog and go around the helo to the other side and stay with the equipment. I'll be there in a minute."

Several hundred yards away on a hillside sat Salazar watching the helicopter being loaded, the wounded in the first one. It took off and the second one landed. He saw Sara with his dog waiting to get on that one. He knew exactly what to do. With one move he would get back at Mr. Steven Hoyt. He turned and slipped quietly down the hill to be closer to them and to get his rocket launcher.

Sara had been sitting on a crate when she decided she wanted to get her backpack out of the cave behind her, so she got up and taking Zeus, slipped between the rocks to where they had prepared to fight only a few hours earlier. She was not sure how Zeus would react, so she took a good tight hold on his leash and stepped into the small clearing. Other than hugging close to her side, he seemed to be okay. She sighed and walked to where her pack lay; her handgun was still tucked into it. She looked through the few other things still there. No weapons, so she turned to head back as the second helicopter lifted off. She stopped and watched as it reached an altitude of a few hundred feet above the trees. Then she watched in horror as the helo was struck midsection by what appeared to be a rocket.

The explosion was deafening as sparks, fire, and bodies fell from the sky. The helicopter spun wildly out of control before crashing a short distance away. Men were yelling; some were screaming in pain. Hondo could not find Sara and was starting to feel his panic rising when she appeared from between the rocks with Zeus close by her side. The rocks had offered her and Zeus enough protection that nothing touched them.

Over the hill, Steve and his men heard the crash. Steve knew what it meant and so did Kurt; they looked at each other, dreading the news but knowing they had to make the call.

Steve held the sat-phone waiting for Hondo to reply; for his part, Hondo knew the question before Steve asked it. "She's okay she was not on board. Repeat, she is okay; she was not on board."

Both men took a brief sigh of relief. "Sit-rep?" Steve asked.

"Not sure, but a couple of guys said they saw a rocket hit it, sir. We are still assessing the damage, sir."

"Do we need to return?"

"We can handle the situation here, sir. You do what you think is best, but between us, I would appreciate you finding the bastard and taking him out!"

Sara looked on at the carnage. She had seen dead animals, and earlier today she saw dead and wounded men, but this was beyond her worst nightmare. *Where do you start to help,* she wondered silently.

"You, get over here." A soldier bending over another man answered her unspoken question.

Sara ran forward, momentarily forgetting Zeus by her side. "Hold this tourniquet, don't let up; if you do, he'll die."

She grabbed the bloody tourniquet and held tight, praying Zeus would behave. He lay quietly at her side, sensing the need to be still.

Over the next few hours, Sara held everything from bloody bandages to the hand of a dying soldier. She had no time for self-reflection, or thoughts of anger, or worry for her dad and Kurt.

The sun was high in the sky when they began the hike down to the waiting Humvees. Salazar did not know he had failed to kill Sara. He immediately went on the run as Steve, Kurt, and their men were on his trail. The third helicopter had taken the wounded and dead out. A small group was left to clean up and wait for more transportation.

Zeus had not left Sara's side. He had settled into just staying close beside her and for the most part not even growling at the men. Of course, to their credit they sort of left him alone since he looked "mean as hell," as one man said.

Sara noted that the men kept her in the center at all times. She prayed that Salazar would not try anything along the trail, for there was no telling how Zeus would react. She said another prayer for Kurt and her father and the men with them. *"Please God, keep them safe."*

For the most part, the hike down to where the Humvees and her Toyota sat was long and uneventful. A couple of the men tripped in the rough terrain with their heavy packs, but no one was seriously injured except maybe a dent in their pride.

Sara checked on the bikes they had left in the cave. Everything appeared to be untouched. Her father and Kurt would probably come this way, so she opted to leave it all. She knew Kurt had watched her disable the truck when they left it and would know where the keys were to the bikes. *At least they will have some transportation at this point,* she thought. Now the most pressing question was, how would Zeus react to the close confines of a Humvee?

They all had a good laugh when Sara climbed in and Zeus jumped in right behind her, promptly taking the seat next to her. One look from him was enough to tell the soldiers that this was his seat and he was not moving!

"We can make this work." Hondo laughed, and then turned to Jake. "You get to sit next to him; I'll be upfront."

"Yes, sir, be happy to, I think, sir," Jake replied with a smile.

Everything went smoothly from that point on. They worked their way down the steep dirt roads to the paved ones and then to the Hoyt Security warehouse.

Chapter Ten

The warehouse was locked up tight, the bollards still in place as she and Kurt had left them. She winced at the thought of him still out there with her father, hunting Salazar. She wanted to get to know him better, a lot better. But the mission they were on was not a safe one; in fact, Salazar would take great delight in killing any and all of them.

She called Billy on one of the sat phones and asked him to open up the gates and drop the bollards; they would be coming in. He was excited to hear from her.

"I can't tell you how happy I am to hear your voice, young lady. I'll be right out," Billy exclaimed.

Billy was more than happy to have Sara back, and to hear her father was alive and safe. "Well, we hope he is still safe," he added.

It was decided that until Kurt, her father, and the other men returned, Sara would be safest at the warehouse compound. It was a defensible area with an entire armory available, and so they waited, and waited and waited. The warehouse was set up with bunks for guys stopping by between jobs. There were showers, a kitchen, and dining hall, and a large game room with a big-screen TV. All in all the men were happy for a place to relax.

Jake, seemed pretty happy with the arrangement; he could not think of an easier way to get to know Sara and maybe turn her easy friendship into something more.

Sara, for her part, was much more interested in controlling Zeus. Other than that, her mind was solely on what was going on at the manhunt several miles away. She found herself trying to analyze her feelings for someone she hardly knew. He had willing put his life on the line for her, and other than her father, no one had ever made her feel like the most important person in the whole world. Her only question was. *Why? Was it to impress her father for a job, or did he care about her?* Those thoughts chased themselves around and around in her mind while they waited for news.

She asked Hondo about the man she had shot. He told her the man would recover and face federal charges. Part of her wondered if there was something wrong with her; *shouldn't she feel bad about shooting someone?* She saw Hondo's men moving on and not dwelling on the skirmish, so she put it in the back of her mind. Later she would talk about it with her father, she decided. Other than that, she kept busy by working with Zeus, sometimes for hours at a time. Zeus, for his part, was a fast and willing learner. He learned her hand signals for nearly every command she could think of. He seemed to know all the basics and responded in both

English and Spanish. She knew he knew to attack on command, she just didn't know the actual verbal command. Jake came up with a possible solution; he went to the base nearby and borrowed a bite-suit so Sara could set Zeus on him.

The day they set everything up, was cool and foggy in the early morning. Jake got into the suit and was glad for the cool morning, as the suit was heavy and hot. Sara asked Jake one last time, "Are you sure you want to do this?"'

"Do it, Sara. Try and see what he does," he said with a confidence he didn't feel.

"Zeus, attack!" Zeus just looked at Sara. "Get him!" Nothing, Zeus cocked his head; he wondered what she wanted him to do. "Well, maybe he doesn't know the command for kill."

"Try Spanish," Jake yelled over to her.

"Zeus, *matar*!"

No sooner was the word out of her mouth than Zeus was leaping toward Jake and attacking him with extreme fury. "Zeus, stop! Come! Down!" Sara started screaming out commands to try to stop him. To his credit Zeus did stop, backing slowly away from Jake toward her and then dropping down.

"Are you all right?" She ran to Jake and was kneeling over him when Kurt and her father drove up. "Oh my God, please answer, are you okay?"

"He just knocked the wind out of me," he managed to wheeze out. "Damn, that was incredible. He hit me like a ton of bricks."

"Sara, what's going on?" Kurt asked, climbing out of the Toyota she had left up the hill days before. The last thing he wanted to see was her bending over another guy when he showed up.

"Kurt! You're back!" She got up and rushed to give him a hug, not caring what he felt for her; she just wanted to be close to him."

"Got one of them for your ole man?" her dad asked, walking up.

"Of course. I am just so glad to see you both." She hugged her father as she had always done when they had been separated for a few days.

Jake, in the meantime, was able to regain his breath and started to get up from his prone position. Zeus stood up and growled, taking a step toward him. "Ah, Sara, you want to call him off now?"

"Zeus, no, down!" Zeus dropped down but never took his eyes off Jake." Wow." She turned back to Kurt and her father. "We were trying to figure out his command for attack. I pretty much have him under control, but we know what he was trained for, so Jake borrowed a suit. You got here just in time to see the results."

"The question is, can you get him to accept Jake again, or is he going to be persona non grata forever more?" Steve asked.

Jake rolled his eyes and pulled off his face guard. "I hope I never look into his eyes like that again. He jumped on my chest and had a hold of this mask and was ripping it off my face! He even bent this thing." He held it up for them to see.

Zeus was standing again. "Zeus, it's all
right, it's Jake." Sara walked over to him and offered her hand to help him to a standing position. "Zeus, come."

Again Zeus did as he was told, but his eyes remained on Jake, and they were not looking at him with love!

"I think I'll get this suit off. It may bring back some bad memories or something." Jake turned to leave. "At least I hope that's all it is." Jake was disappointed. He had spent all the time and effort he could the last few days trying to get Sara to look at him the way she looked at Kurt, but to no avail.

"So what happened? Did you get Salazar?" Sara turned back to Kurt and her father.

"No, as far as we can tell he went home," Kurt answered. He was feeling better now that Jake had left the area. "We tracked him down the hill into

Sacramento, and then we alerted the authorities to watch for him between there and Mexico, and the next we hear he was spotted in his hometown. He managed to sneak across the border somehow. So we think we are good for now."

Sara looked to each of them. "So I can go home? I mean really Dad, I like this place but I like home better."

"I think so, hon. We need to be on guard though. If I were a gambling man, I would bet money that his plan was to kill or maim you in the chopper. What we don't know is if he knows he missed. But I can tell you right now he will be back as soon as he finds out you are still alive and well."

"I thought about that, Daddy."
She looked at him knowingly. "I've had
a lot of time to think the last few days! I
had walked around to the other side of
the chopper from where the rocket was
launched, I got up at the last minute and
went inside the little area where we
stayed. I looked up as the chopper took
off and then watched as the rocket came
up and hit it. He might not have been
able to see that I was in the little
compound area, so he may have thought
I was on it."

"I can't tell you what Kurt and I
went through for a few minutes. Sorry,
Kurt, I should not have spoken for you, "
Steve apologized.

Kurt looked at him and then at
Sara. "Are you kidding? My heart

stopped and I couldn't breathe until Hondo said 'She's okay!' Sorry, Sara, but I really do care about you, and I know you haven't known me long, but, honestly, do you think you could put a guy out of his misery and tell me I have a chance?"

After the last few days of wondering how he felt, Sara was so relieved that she practically leaped into his arms and kissed him quickly, directly on the mouth. "You got a really good chance, big guy!"

He quickly wrapped his arms around her and found her lips again, regardless of who was watching. He was praying her dad would approve. The rest of the guys that had now filed outside to welcome them back could be damned.

The loud cheers and backslapping were enough to bring them both back to reality.

"Sorry, sir, I should have said something to you first," he apologized to Steve.

"No worries, son. I have known almost from the first moment I saw you two together." He looked over at Sara and grinned. "I just hope you realize how much of handful she can be!"

"Daddy!" She laughed at him.

Chapter Eleven

The next few weeks were the best that Sara could remember in a long time. It wasn't as if she had a bad life before Kurt, it was just that something had been missing. That something was Kurt; they spent nearly all day everyday together, talking, sharing, and both in wonder at it all.

Sara learned about Kurt's family, how he had grown up on his family's ranch. She shared how she had been on her great-grandpa's horse ranch until she was about eight. How it had been her and her dad ever since her mom had been killed in an accident when she was four, and how her dad had always done his best to be there for her. How he would take her with him to business meetings, and she would sit in the corner and draw or read while he conducted meetings.

Steve, for his part, was worried Salazar would find out she was still alive and would come back, he was sure of it. They had his son and he wanted revenge; he had wanted it way too long to suddenly give up. All their sources were sure Salazar was in Mexico, but Steve knew firsthand that would not stop him. He told Sara and Kurt to be careful, to not get so distracted that they missed something, but he remembered how Sara's mom had made him feel when they met, and he knew it was nearly impossible.

Sara was still bothered by having shot a man, but the scene in the mountains did not seem to be weighing on either Kurt or Steve. She was sitting on the beach looking particularly pensive. Zeus was lying next to her with his head in her lap, when Kurt came up to her after taking a swim in the ocean." What's wrong?" he asked.

Sara shook her head slightly. "Nothing, I'm fine."

"You don't look fine. Come on, please, tell me. Maybe I can help." He knelt down next to her.

She paused for a moment and then said, "I keep thinking, I shot someone, and then; nothing. I am not questioned, I," she paused, "I don't even know if he lived or died, and my life has just gone on like nothing happened, except I have Zeus now." She scratched the dog's neck lovingly. Zeus cuddled closer.

Kurt responded, "First of all, I know it got to me the first time I had to shoot someone in combat. I think that if it doesn't bother you, that's when you should worry. At the same time, you didn't seek out someone to shoot. That man was commanding his dog to attack us, and he had every intention of killing or maiming us. I thank God your daddy prepared and trained you to protect yourself; we might not be here if you had not shot him. Sooner or later, when he goes on trial, you'll probably be called on to testify, unless he cuts a deal or they have enough evidence on him without you." He reached out and took one of her hands in his. "You did the right thing, Sara. It's not pretty, it's not a game, but you did the right thing."

"Thank you. I just kept thinking that could not be the end of it." She sighed. "Thank you."

You can always come to me, tell me anything, except, go away," he added with a grin.

"Ditto." She laughed, happy he did not want to go anywhere.

Kurt was glad she was finally feeling like she could talk to him. She was always so reserved, like she was holding back somehow, not quite willing to go all in with him.

The following morning Kurt went to Steve. "Sir, you have been very gracious to let me stay here, to spend time with Sara, but I need to earn my keep, sir. I came here for a job. I need to do something. I could go home to Texas, but right now. . . ."

Steve interrupted. "First of all, you will be paid for all this. I'm sorry I've been distracted dealing with everything, but it's been a relief having you with Sara." He held up his hand when Kurt would have interrupted him. "I know you care about Sara and you would protect her with your life without being paid, but you will be taken care of. Secondly, Sara told me about your family's ranch in Texas, and I'm guessing that you want to end up there, but your heart is right here in California?"

"Yes, sir. I want to ask Sara to marry me, but all I can offer her right now is a place on my family's ranch in

Texas, and I don't think she would be happy that far from you."

"Your family has a pretty good size ranch in Texas?" Steve asked, realizing that the little he knew about Kurt was what they had talked about. Normally he would have run a background check on him by now, but with all that had gone on the last few weeks, he had overlooked it.

"Yes, sir. I'm not sure about the size any more. Dad and Kevin, that's my older brother, have bought out a few smaller spreads that wanted out, but they have also sold some acreage when it served. I think we are over a hundred-thousand acres that we own. We run cattle on some of it, and lease out some, and then there is more acreage that is free range. I could go back and just ranch with my dad and family, or, my uncle is the local sheriff, he always wanted me to be one of his deputies. He is how I met Paul Jensen, which is how I came to be here."

"What makes you so sure Sara would not be happy with you in Texas?" Steve asked, a sick feeling rising in his throat, realizing he was on the verge of losing his little girl.

"Sir, you are pretty much her only family. I'm sure she would try, but I would rather give up on the ranch than lose her."

"She might feel the same way, son. She might be willing to give up her life here because you would be happier there."

"I don't want to risk it, sir. I want her to be happy, no matter what."

"Why did you come to me in the first place, for a job, that is?"

"I thought I could work for you for a year or so and re-acclimate back into civilian life, then go home. I honestly didn't plan on meeting Sara. I don't suppose you would be interested in moving your headquarters to Texas?" Kurt asked jokingly.

"Well. . ." Steve smiled, somewhat relieved that Kurt wanted him to stay close to Sara. "That's an idea, but I'd like to see the two of you together for awhile first." He held up his hand again to stop Kurt from replying. "Trust me, I know how you feel. I fell hard for her mom the first time I laid eyes on her, and there has never been anyone else. It's a long story, but Sandi never fit into the D.C. political scene. She tried, but backstabbing and backroom deals were not her style. I was trying to talk her into moving back to California, and I would commute back and forth until my term was over. She was adamantly against it, and then her grandpa got hurt; it was pretty serious. It was only then that I managed to convince her to move back home to help him and Nan, and I followed her back out to California when my term in Congress was up. Like you, I would have given up anything to keep her happy. I rewrote my life for Sandi and Sara, and I would happily do so again, Kurt. Let's just let this play out for a few more weeks. I am still concerned about Salazar. We still have his boy, and when he finds out Sara is still alive, if he doesn't know already, I am not thinking he will be pleased."

Kurt got a sinking feeling." She said she was going to the grocery store this morning; maybe I shouldn't have let her go alone." He looked down at Zeus lying nearby." She doesn't even have Zeus with her."

"It's probably just me worrying, but maybe you should check on her."

"Me too!" Kurt replied, pulling out his phone and calling her. 'No answer, it went straight to voicemail. I think I will go over there. Can I borrow your car?"

Steve tossed him a set of keys. "Go, and call me when you get with her."

Ten minutes earlier, Sara had entered the grocery store. She liked shopping early in the morning. There were fewer people, and Kurt had said he wanted to talk with her father that morning. She had let her mind wander about what and why, as she looked around after grabbing a cart. She was headed down the first aisle when suddenly the lights went out. She heard an announcement over the intercom. "Ms. Sara Hoyt, please come to the back entrance to the store. Do not try to escape. I have people at every door. They are all armed, and they will start shooting hostages if you do not do as I say. If you do what you are told, you have a chance of living and so do they. If not . . . well, you decide who lives and who dies."

Sara's blood ran cold. She felt like she could hardly breathe. Her chest was frozen in fear. She knew by the accent who was talking. She remembered what her father had said. "Don't let him take you alive," but what about the others, could she just let other people die? Her thoughts chased themselves around in her mind. Her phone was in her pocket. She took it out and started to send a text. "I would not do that, señorita. Just go and meet with Señor Salazar." She felt the cold barrel of a gun against the back of her neck. Sara walked calmly, much more calmly than she felt, to the back of the store. Something stung in her neck, and then as blackness overtook her, she heard an automatic gun going off and people screaming.

Steve's phone rang a few minutes later. "So she's fine, right?"

"Sir, you had better get down here. There are at least five dead and I don't know how many wounded. There are cops everywhere, and they won't let me in to see what happened. I don't know if she's here or not!"

Steve was there in minutes, but to Kurt it felt like hours. He had finally found Paul Jensen. It seemed that mass shootings brought out the head of the local police force. The two of them met Steve when he arrived. "I can't find her. The one survivor we talked with said he thought Salazar took her out the back door. We are trying to get the security footage now and see if we can find out what kind of vehicle he had." Paul was trying to fill Steve in quickly. He knew him, and he knew that Steve was going to do whatever was necessary to get information as quickly as possible.

To Steve's credit, his years of training took over and he took a deep breath. "How long ago did all this happen? We need to shut off all roads out of here. If he gets away, there is no telling what he will do to her."

"Already ordered. Any ideas as to why he wants her?" Paul asked.

"To punish me and to get his kid back," Steve responded, and then he looked at Kurt. "Don't think about what he might do. We need to find him. Get your head on, son."

Kurt took a breath. "Yes sir. I have an idea, sir."

"Shoot!" Steve responded.

"Get on the news. Offer to trade Salazar's son for Sara, unhurt in any way!"

"I don't have the authority to make that trade. I know who does, but I'm not sure if I can convince him or not."

"Salazar does not know that, sir. The sooner we reach out, the sooner we can try to stop him from torturing her."

"The kid's got a decent idea, Steve. If we can pull it off, we may be able to get ahead of this."

A few miles away, Sara came to, lying face down on a cold cement floor. Her only clothes were her bra and panties. She looked around and could see she was in a sort of chain-link cage, no blanket, only a five-gallon bucket in the corner, which she assumed would be for her to relieve herself in. The cage appeared to be in a large warehouse, and even though the cage itself was brightly lit, she could barely see any details beyond the chain-link, as all the windows were blacked out except for the highest ones.

She sat up slowly. Her head hurt, and she was stiff and sore from lying on the hard, cold concrete floor.

"Stand up, bitch," she heard from somewhere off to the side.

Sara didn't really feel much like complying, but on the other hand, she didn't want things to get worse. "I'm not bitch; the name is Sara. "She was surprised that her voice sounded calmer than she felt.

"I want to see you. I think you may be more valuable to sell off to one of my friends than to torture to death. Besides, then your daddy can wonder and fret and worry and wonder some more about what happened to you. That might be better than the joy of killing you."   His wicked, sick laughter was enough to make her blood run cold.

In spite of her fear, anger bubbled up inside Sara and she tamped it down. She remembered what her father had told her ever since she was little; "When you lose your temper, you quit thinking, then you lose the battle'. She took a deep breath and stood up. It was humiliating, standing there in her underwear being ogled by at least half a dozen men. They were whistling. She wanted to cower, but years of talking with guys from Special Forces and her dad made her straighten her back and stand tall and defiant.

She could see him now; he had walked closer to her cage. "You know, Salazar, I thought you were a smart man, evil, but I never took you for stupid."

She had touched a nerve. His nostrils flared. "I am not stupid. I have you in a cage. You, are the stupid one."

"You have a young woman in a cage, someone that is not nearly as strong physically as yourself, and you are surrounded by at least six other strong and well-armed men. That's your big accomplishment? How many people do you think are out looking for me? You kidnapped the daughter of a freaking retired US congressman and

Navy SEAL; you think that was smart?" *Where did all that come from*, she asked herself. Maybe she shouldn't bait him; she might make things worse. "Go to hell, Salazar!" She turned and walked to the corner with the bucket; she flipped it upside down and sat on it.

"You are a scrappy little thing, I will give you that, but the bravado will soon go away. Soon you will be begging me for food and water." He turned and started to walk away.

"I am sure I will be worth more money if I am starved and can barely walk," she said sarcastically. A thought came to her. "You know, you could trade me for your son."

He stopped for a moment and then kept walking away, followed by his entourage of men.

Sara hoped she had given him some food for thought; hopefully, he would give her food and water. She had to keep her strength up and not let fear take over her mind; being sold as a sex slave was not an enticing thought. *Please God, show Kurt and Daddy where I am. Please help them find me.*

She got up and walked around the cage. Bolted to the floor, it had chain-link on all sides and the top. Escape without some bolt cutters and tools did not look promising.

Chapter Twelve

Steve had been making calls for the last couple of hours, all the way up the chain of command to the attorney general of the US; no one was terribly excited about doing a trade. The most he got from the top man himself was he would consider it as a last resort, but "no promises."

Paul and Kurt were sitting with Steve waiting for the last call to finish. Paul spoke first. "They found the van we saw in the security footage, burned to a crisp. We have no idea what they transferred her into. I have men combing traffic cams and security cams to try to get a clue."

Steve shook his head as if to clear his thoughts. "Thanks, Paul. I know you are doing all you can. Kurt, if you were to take someone and knew you could not get out of town, where would you take her?"

Kurt scoffed and shook his head. "I don't know, a warehouse, a safe house, maybe a boat off shore."

"We have the Coast Guard monitoring and searching every boat leaving the area, no matter how small." Paul spoke up again.

"A warehouse where there are very few cameras. The old district, there are a couple of old warehouses that are empty, "Steve quietly stated, then he turned to Paul. "We need to get a hold of Mike Rodriquez. He's the head of the local DEA."

"Yeah I know, but why?" Paul asked.

"We need him, your local drug guys, and a warrant when we find what we need. One of those warehouses just might be where she is. Salazar has a drug trade here. He gets a lot of it in off the ocean, small fishing boats that get by the Coast Guard without a second look. The warehouse would need to be right on the water, where they could bring in the shipments, sort the drugs, and ship them out. That was a good idea, Kurt. Paul, can you get your people to look up ownership of every one of the warehouses down at the wharf? It'll probably be held by a shell corp., but have them check for anything that is even slightly hinky. Kurt, do you think you can handle Zeus?"

"Maybe, he's been pretty good at doing what I ask the last few weeks, but Sara can override anything I say."

"That dog adores her, and his ability to smell may be our greatest asset. Start by taking a drive with the windows down; go down by the wharf and see if he reacts at all. I have a feeling that if she is anywhere that he can pick up her scent, he will, and he will let you know. If he reacts at all, bring him back and we will get a plan together. Do not try to go in alone, please," he added forcefully. "I mean it, Kurt. Don't try it alone. I am going to get a hold of the guys that helped us out before. I want them standing by. Between Paul's people, the DEA, the guys from Homeland, and us, we should have a fighting chance at a rescue; if we can locate her."

Kurt was skeptical but at the same time happy to have something to do beside sitting and waiting.

He called Zeus, who came willingly enough but not with the same enthusiasm as when Sara called him." Come on, boy; let's go see if we can find her." He turned back to Paul and Steve. "Either of you know where I can borrow a kid's car with super dark windows? That way if does Salazar see us he won't see Zeus. All I have to do is crack the window for Zeus to use his nose, but he won't be able to jump out and alert him."

Paul got up. "Come on, we should have something in the yard for undercover work."

Hours slipped by; Steve made phone calls and started putting a plan together.   He even convinced the attorney general to let him move Salazar's son close and start negotiating a trade with Salazar should he be able to make contact. They did not want him to suggest a trade on the news, or every criminal with clout would try something similar. He knew this part of the job was essential to any successful operation, but he really wanted to be out looking for Sara.   He kept telling himself; *you've tried to teach her what to do and how to handle a situation like this. If anyone can survive, she can.*

Chapter Thirteen

It was a short while later that one of Salazar's men brought her a bottle of water and an apple. "You stay back while I put this in," he said with a deep accent.

Sara complied. Not only had her head not stopped hurting, her stomach had been growling for the last hour or so, and there was a really sore spot on her neck that seemed to be getting worse by the minute. She hoped the water and food would help. Something she had said must have made sense to Salazar; he was not going to let her starve or die of dehydration.

A little while later, Sara was not sure how long, maybe hours, her head was hurting really badly, and she ached all over, the little man was back again. "You get back. I give you this to wear. Señor Salazar, he said, it will make you more attractive to the buyers, and no bra. You remove. "He smiled a wicked smile, and his stained yellow teeth showed. Then he put the clothes in her cage and walked away laughing.

Buyers, great, then I am to be sold. Well, I hope that fate is better than being tortured to death, she thought. She walked over to the small pile of material on the floor and picked it up. A very lightweight, skintight dress, well, some would call it that. It was split to the navel in front, below the lower back in the rear, and up both sides from the bottom. *Wow, this can hardly be called clothes. Definitely not my style,* she thought. *I feel more covered in my underwear.* She knew they were watching all the time. It was the most humiliating thing she had ever had to do, but she slipped on the dress and did her best to not show off her breasts when she took off her bra. From the catcalls and whistles she heard in the distance, she knew she had pretty much failed. She looked up at the camera and yelled, "Bring me a comb so I can comb my hair, please, and a way to wash my face and hands."

Salazar watched on the screen in the office a few buildings away. He turned to one of his men. "Take her a comb and a way to clean up. We want her to look nice for the bidders."

Sara cleaned up, then. She parted her long blond hair on one side, bringing the other side forward, covering as much of her face as she could. She was beginning to think something was seriously wrong with her neck. It seemed to be swelling, and she was pretty sure she was now running a fever.

Meanwhile, Kurt drove up and down every street down by the wharf, in and out of all the side streets. It seemed like hours before Zeus stood up and acted like he smelled her. Then he sat down again within a few moments. "Is she in there. Boy?" Kurt asked him while scratching his neck. "Seek, Zeus, seek. We'll go down to the end of the street and come back again."

Again, when they were close to the same area, Zeus stood up. This time he whined as well. "Okay boy, let's get her daddy and get her out of there." Kurt drove straight back to the command center where Steve and Paul were.

"I think we may have found . . ." His voice faded when he saw the way they were watching a computer screen. It was video of Sara. "What the hell?"

Steve immediately turned to him, trying to get him to turn around. "Wait outside, Kurt; you don't need to see this."

Kurt pushed his hand back; he felt like he had been kicked in the gut. "No, I need to know what's going on. Is this live?"

"No, they shut off the feed a few minutes ago. We're just trying to see if we can tell anything." Steve turned back to the screen." Can you zoom in on her hands? What did you say when you came in, Kurt?"

While the computer operator readjusted the playback, Kurt replied, "I think I know which warehouse she's in. It was the only one Zeus reacted to at all. It's really big, and it's right on the waterfront. All the windows down at the lower levels are blacked out. We did not stop, sir. We just rolled by twice. The first time Zeus stood up, but the second time, he was on the same side as the warehouse, and he stood up and put his nose to the window and whined. I think she's in there."

"Here you go sir, her hands," the computer operator said.

"Good work, Kurt," Steve turned back to the screen. "Alright, that's my girl." Steve said slowly, "Warehouse . . . sea . . . cage . . . booby-trap. . . trade . . . trap . . . Salazar . . . not . . . here. She's trying to tell us anything she can with her index finger. Watch it, she's going through the same thing over and over. It's Morse code. I taught her that when she was about ten or twelve. Warehouse, sea, cage, booby-trap, trade, trap, Salazar not here."

"So she is in a warehouse by the sea in a cage, and the cage is booby-trapped?" Kurt went through it. "We thought she was in a warehouse, and we know from the video that she is in a cage; it all fits." His voice shook. "She's amazing. When I saw her, it looked like her hair was down over her face. Why? Do you think he beat her?"

Steve had wondered the same thing. Aloud he answered, "Maybe, but maybe she is trying to make sure that it will be hard to recognize her when this is all over. That's a good sign. It means she hasn't given up; she's thinking of surviving this. Paul, we need to get everyone together and get the plan going. I am not sure what she meant by 'trade, trap,' unless she thinks Salazar is going to set up a trade and then pull a fast one and still sell her. We need to be prepared for almost anything."

Sara prayed that her father would see the video, She had not been quite prepared, She was not let out of the cage; they had just filmed her right there. When she asked one of the men where Salazar was, why he was not watching her humiliation, he told her that, "Señor Salazar is watching from his office down the street, but he knows what you are doing. He can see everything, and with the push of button, boom, no more **señorita**. "He shook his head sadly but then laughed and laughed as he walked away.

Kurt listened to the plans being laid out for Sara's rescue, and tried not to let his anger take over He kept telling himself, *if she can keep her head, then so can I.* They were all trying to think of different traps Salazar could set up. "Sir, she said 'Salazar not here.' Where do you think he could be, close?"

"Possibly. I don't think he would go back to Mexico, not yet. I'm not sure he ever did. Why?"'

"When we drove away from the warehouse, we drove past another

182

building and Zeus growled, I thought he was just mad that we were leaving, but maybe he was trying to tell me where Salazar was."

"Show me the building." When Kurt pointed it out on the satellite picture of the area they thought she was in, Steve turned to one of the other men. "Let's pull the building plans on these buildings, see if there is a way for Salazar to get between the buildings without coming out onto the street. Is there a sewer, or utility area under the street there?"

Chapter Fourteen

Other than the filming of her video, Sara was left alone and the time dragged by. She could tell that it was getting dark by the uncovered window high up on the walls; she could see the light was slowly fading. She tried to remember how long she had been here, but her mind did not want to focus. Her body ached, and she felt cold to her core. There was still no blanket. The light above her cage never went out or dimmed; it stayed on brightly shining down on her, every minute of the day and now the night. She had spent her time walking around in circles, checking each nook and cranny of her cage. She thought there was C-4 on one side of the cage, but she was not sure, and she was so tired, too tired, and weak to even think. She sat down in the corner and eventually fell over, passed out. When the guard that brought her food came he could not wake her, and he ran all the way back to the office to tell his boss.

He knew that it was bad. The beautiful girl was in a very bad way; he could feel the heat in her body, when he went into the cage to wake her. She felt hot through her clothes, and she was barely breathing.

At first Salazar did not believe the young guard, but he looked at the screen in his office. She was not moving.

"La fiebre, la fiebre, muy caliente!" The guard kept repeating.

Salazar really didn't care if she died, but not yet. He needed her alive until he got his son back and that would not be tonight. He had sent a message to Mr. Steven Hoyt that, "he would trade his daughter for his son." Salazar told the guard to return to watch her; he would get a doctor to check her out.

Sara faded in and out of consciousness when the doctor examined her. He knew her condition was dangerously bad. Her fever was over 104, her heartbeat was irregular, her blood pressure was dangerously low, and there was a large swelling on the side of her neck that seemed to be growing by the minute. Salazar wanted her alive until tomorrow morning; he was not sure he could make that happen. He was not even sure she would be alive in the morning if he had her in a hospital.

"You must get her off this floor and into a bed. I am going to setup an IV of antibiotics. She has an infection, and it appears to be very strong. My only hope is that she is not allergic to anything I am giving her," the doctor told Salazar. "She belongs in a hospital. I am not sure we can keep her alive until morning."

"I certainly hope you are wrong, Doctor. I need her to be able to walk tomorrow morning! Your life may very well depend on her being alive; do you understand me?"

The doctor shook his head. He was not sure what to do. The man expected miracles. Her being alive was unlikely, and her walking even less.

Chapter Fifteen

The morning dawned damp and foggy as it often does along the shore. The night had been a busy one, with no sleep for anyone involved except Sara. Though she had slept, her sleep had not been restful. Her fever still raged, her neck looked like a growth had developed on the side, and she was having difficulty breathing.

"Señorita." The little guard that had brought her an apple and water the day before, shook her gently. "Señorita, you must wake up." He shook her arm; he could feel how hot her fevered body was through the blanket covering her. He saw how flushed her face was. He shook her again. "Por favor, you must get up."

She pushed his hand away and tried to sit up, only to fall back, almost blacking out. "I can't!" She croaked out, not recognizing her own voice.

"You must. You are to be traded to your papa for Señor Salazar's son. You must get up now!" He urged her, seemingly genuinely.

She tried to gather her thoughts. Kurt and her father were going to trade for her? But how, who, for Salazar's son? Her mind would not focus; she kept feeling like she would black out when she moved. With all the fortitude she could muster, she forced herself into a sitting position. The room seemed to spin around like a carnival ride at a dizzying speed.

She was still in the "dress" she had worn for the video. She felt exposed and unable to cover herself. She forced herself to try to stand, and the little guard took her arm to help her up. The room spun even faster as she struggled to gain her balance. *What is wrong with me*, she asked herself. Her neck hurt, and she put her hand up and felt the tennis ball size swelling. It hurt so badly when she touched it, she wondered if she was going to lose consciousness again. *This is not good,* she thought. *I need to warn them.* Then her mind wandered. *Warn them of what? Warn who?* Try as she might, she was barely able to focus and put one foot in front of the other.

The guard wrapped a blanket around her, and with his help she walked out of the cage to a black SUV parked a few feet away.

The drive was a blur. Sara could not tell what direction they went or how far they drove.

"Wake her up!" Salazar commanded. "She has to walk, or this will not work."

"I am trying. She is very sick, Señor, very, very sick."

The guard helped her out of the SUV when they stopped. She forced herself to stand on her own, and with every ounce of strength she could muster, she slowly put one foot in front of the other and walked in the direction they told her. "Stop!"Salazar commanded. She stood, swaying slightly, trying to stay upright. "Where is my son?" She heard him yell at someone. She tried to get her eyes to focus but could only see fuzzy figures, in the distance.

"He is here." She heard her father's voice. Was Kurt with him? A dog barked. *Zeus?* She wondered, but her eyes would not focus, "Let her go, Salazar. I don't know what you have done to her, but let her go now or the deal is off."

"You send my son and she can go."

Steve knew Salazar had no intention of releasing her. His ear bud crackled to life. "You're clear, sir. We have them."

"Sara, down!" he yelled, which he really had not needed to do as she was already falling, having lost consciousness. In the distance she heard shots, a dog barking, yelling men, and then silence.

Steve turned to Kurt." Let him go."

Kurt had already released Zeus as he himself began running toward Sara. It had taken all his will power to wait as long as he had. A sniper's bullet had dropped Salazar, but Zeus did not care. Sara was down, and he felt that Salazar had taken another mistress away. He attacked the body of Salazar with a vengeance that most had never seen.

Kurt reached Sara. He could tell she was alive but in very bad shape. He yelled for an ambulance and called Zeus, who released his hold on Salazar and came back to his and Sara's side. Zeus nudged his mistress with his nose and whined at her.

"She's going to be all right, buddy." Kurt scratched the dog's neck and reassured him; hoping he was not wrong.

When the ambulance sped away a short time later Kurt and Steve watched it go: both silently praying they were not too late. They knew Sara was extremely ill, and running a dangerously high fever.

Chapter Sixteen

It was hours before they could get any news on Sara. Besides having to get through what they had to handle at the scene, the doctors had Sara first in the ER and then in ICU, and all they could get news of is that they were trying to get her fever down.

Finally, a nurse came out paging the Hoyt family.   Steve, Kurt, Paul Jensen, and Zeus all stood up. "Right here," Steve responded.

"The dog cannot come in, sir. I'm sorry." The nurse looked at them all like they had taken leave of their senses bringing a dog into the hospital.

"He's a service dog. He is your patient's service dog, and it is important that she knows he is okay and that he knows she is okay. We will take him out as soon as we can," Steve responded, with a look and tone that indicated there would be hell to pay for not just going about her business.

"I . . ."

"Just get the doctor so we can get some answers, and we will get out of your hair." Again Steve's voice commanded respect and obedience.

With that, she turned and hurried off down the hall. A doctor appeared a few moments later. "Mr. Hoyt?"

"Yes, I am Mr. Hoyt." The steeliness in his voice was all that showed his impatience.

"Are these family members?" she asked, looking at Paul and Kurt and patently ignoring Zeus.

"This, ma'am, is the chief of police, and this is my daughter's fiancé, and her service dog. Please, just tell us that you know what is wrong with her and that she going to be okay before this young man and I have a meltdown."

She nodded, "It's touch and go right now. She has an extremely bad infection; we have her on IV antibiotics. I was coming to you to see if we can perform a minor surgery to drain the swelling on her neck. We believe it is an abscess, and it is affecting her breathing. I would like to try to drain it rather than intubate her. It is a minor procedure, but I do believe it is vital to her getting well."

Steve looked to Kurt, who nodded almost imperceptibly. "Do it. How soon will we be able to see her? She is going to be in pretty bad shape emotionally when she comes around. I want to be sure she knows she is safe."

The doctor looked at the three of them with a new understanding. "She is the girl that was kidnapped at the grocery store the other day?"

"Yes," Paul answered, "and it is imperative we see her as soon as she is conscious."

The doctor sighed, "I understand. Please, there is an empty meeting room down this way. Perhaps you all can wait in it until we can get her feeling better."

Hours dragged by, Kurt took Zeus for a walk every couple of hours, each time hoping for some word of Sara's condition by the time he returned. It was nearly dinnertime before the doctor entered the room. "Sorry, it took a little longer than I anticipated for Miss Hoyt to start responding to our efforts. She is still not conscious; but she should be coming around anytime. Mr. Hoyt, your daughter was very near death when she arrived. I believe we are past the worst of it, and now it is just a matter of giving her time to start healing."

"That's great news. We would like to be with her when she comes around. Can you arrange that?" Steve responded his relief showed clearly in his voice.

"I have her in a corner room in the ICU department. The hospital is not big on having a lot of visitors in that area, but we are going to make an exception in this case. Please follow me."

"Steve, you and Kurt go ahead. I need to talk to her as soon as she is able, but I can wait some," Paul told them. "I'm going to head back to the office and do some catch-up."

"Thanks, Paul. Means a lot, you waiting with us." Steve shook Paul's hand before turning back and following the doctor.

"Yes, thanks, Paul. Without you I would have probably been arrested at the scene!" Kurt added, shaking Paul's hand before following Steve and the doctor.

It was still a couple of hours before Sara came around. She was pale and looked like she had lost weight in the short time since the men had seen her. Her eyes fluttered, and she moaned softly before opening her eyes completely. Kurt's smiling face was the first thing she saw. "Oh, thank God, you found me!" That was all she could croak out.

"You're safe, babe, you are safe. Just rest and get well." He held her hand softly. Zeus jumped up on the side of the bed and laid his head on her arm.

"Zeus, you're okay, boy. Where's Dad?"

"Right here, honey. We are all right here. The hospital is going to kick us all out pretty soon. They want you to rest."

A look of compete panic swept over Sara's face. "No, please don't leave." Her voice was still raspy, but the panic came through loud and clear to both the men.

"Okay, no worries, one of us will stay here with you. You won't be alone." Steve comforted her, turning to Kurt. "You take first watch; I'll take Zeus and go home and shower, clean up, and try to grab a couple hours sleep. When I get back you can do the same. Okay with you?"

"Yes, sir. Thank you; I don't really want to leave her right now."

Chapter Seventeen

Sara was awake when Steve returned in the morning.   She still looked tired and weak, but at least she was awake.

"Hi, Daddy," she managed weakly, her voice still hoarse.

Kurt looked like he hadn't gotten much sleep. A couple days' growth of beard made him look even more haggard. "Morning, sir."

Zeus was overjoyed that his mistress was moving at all. He immediately jumped on the bed next to Sara and lay down, pushing as close to her as he could. Sara smiled, and laid her hand on his head. "Did you miss me, Zeus baby?"

"We can both answer that one," Steve replied dryly. "I've never seen a depressed dog before this." He turned to Kurt, "Go get some rest, Kurt. Here are keys to the house; you know the code. Car is parked a few spaces down from where we parked yesterday, and take the mutt with you. I am pretty sure we are pushing the limits of the hospital's patience with him here."

"Thank you, sir. Come o, Zeus. See you later, babe." He bent over and gave Sara a quick kiss on the forehead. Zeus had ignored him. "Zeus, come."

"Zeus, go with Kurt. You can come back later." Sara talked to him like he could understand every word and Zeus seemed to respond accordingly.

Sara waited until Kurt had left before turning to her father. "Please, Daddy, tell me what happened. How did you rescue me? How did you know what happened to me? From the beginning please," she begged weakly.

"Okay, I'll go over everything, but if you get upset or if you're too tired, I quit, agreed?" She nodded her agreement and then winced as her neck hurt when she moved. "Kurt and I were talking that morning. I told him I was concerned that Salazar might find out you were still alive, and come after you.

205

He said you had gone to the store, and you were alone, so out of concern for you he went to the store. Neither of us really believed Salazar would actually try to get you at the store, maybe at home, on the beach, something like that, but in the middle of a busy store in broad daylight? I'm sorry, I underestimated him. That cost several people their lives, and you nearly lost yours."

"Salazar shot a bunch of people at the store, didn't he?"

"Yes, all in all five died, and ten more were wounded. I just wish I would have realized what he planned."

"I'm sorry. I should have followed your training, and maybe none of this would have happened," she replied.

"I hope you don't mean that you would've rather killed yourself than be captured. I, for one, am glad you—"

"No, no," she interrupted. "I should have followed all your self-defense training and taken the gun away from the guy that took me to Salazar, and shot my way out of the store. The only reason I went with him is I thought I was saving the people at the store. As I was passing out, I thought I heard shots. I asked one of the nurses when Kurt was getting some coffee; the nurse told me what he had heard from the news. I was trying to save lives, not cost them."

"You can't blame yourself. You can, however, blame Salazar. He's the one who did it!" He scolded her.

"You either," she tossed back.

"You must be feeling better, using my words against me!" He laughed. " Okay, we can't change the past. Anyway, after you were taken, Paul helped us with locking down the city, and we starting looking for where Salazar might be hiding you. It was Kurt and Zeus that figured it out. Kurt drove all over down by the docks with Zeus. He is a really good dog, honey; I'm glad we saved him. Zeus indicated which warehouse you were in, and Kurt came back to tell me. It was at that point we were analyzing the video."

"Oh jeez, I was mortified. That piece of cloth hardly covered anything. The only thing I prayed was that you would see me signaling you."

"'I did. That was all that kept us from rushing in. Had we, who knows what would have happened? Salazar had enough C-4 on one side of your cage to bring down that whole warehouse and half the block. But, you got really sick, and that was when Salazar reached out to me to try to pull off a trade for his son. By the time he contacted me, Hondo and his group had arrived. We set a trap, and Salazar walked into it."

"How did you convince the government to give you Salazar's son?"

"Didn't; Hondo is about the same size and build as his son. We put a hood over his head, and he pretended to be his son. We rigged the shackles to spring loose, and Hondo had a gun in his hands behind his back. When I yelled 'down' to you, Hondo dropped to the ground and came up shooting. We were sure Salazar was going to try to shoot you. Hondo dropped him with his first shot, a sniper hit him with a second shot, or maybe it was vice versa. As he was falling, Zeus hit him full force in the chest. The man did not have a chance."

"Wow, I hope you thanked Hondo for me. Thank you for telling me. I don't think Kurt was too keen on telling me. "Her voice seemed weak, and she had to force her eyes open. "But now I have a couple more questions. Salazar sold me, he said to one of his Iranian friends. Is that guy going to come looking for his purchase? And what about Salazar's son? Is he going to be looking for more revenge? Is he going to blame us, me, you, or Kurt for not only his grandpa's death, but now his papa's death?"

"Possibly. We don't know what he'll do when he hears. He's being held in super-max, and there is not much chance of him getting out for a long time. We can't live in fear, though. We just have to be watchful, and live our lives, enjoying each day."

She smiled. "You used to tell me that worrying about something takes the joy away from the now."

"That was something your mother taught me; live each day as if it is your last, no regrets. Hard to do sometimes, but it is the best I can tell you. Now I have a question for you."

"Okay, what?"

"Did Kurt ask you to marry him? And what was your answer?"

"That's cheating." She stalled. "That's two questions." She sighed. "Yes, he did ask me, and I have not answered him. I don't feel right marrying him with this Salazar thing still hanging over my head."

"Do you love him?"

"You know I do."

"Then you need to marry him and get as much joy as you can each and every day. Don't waste time with what-ifs. Life is too short, honey. You need to live it, enjoy it. We never know how much time we have. Even though I only had a few years with your mama, I was never sorry for what we had. Sorry that we didn't have more, absolutely, but I would not have given up any time we had," he advised her.

"What about you? What will you do if we move to Texas?"

"Well, probably I'll have to move somewhere nearby so I can see my grandkids!" He replied without missing a beat.

"Really? You would really move to Texas?"

"Honestly, Kurt already asked if I would. I haven't had much time to think about it, but an old friend of mine is in the Cattlemen's Association down there; once before he offered me a job. I think I can be close enough that we will both feel good about it, without being too close. Okay?"

"Thank you, Daddy. As usual, you find a way to solve my problems."

"That's all well and good, but henceforth you need to trust Kurt. He loves you, and his first concern is your happiness. Okay?"

"Okay! But Daddy, if Salazar's son, I don't even know his name, does come after us, are we putting Kurt's family in danger, especially if we go there?"

"His name is Alexandro, and that is a possibility, but you need to remember a couple of things. Like I said, he's in super-max. We are going to make it as difficult as possible for him to get the word out to do anything, and whether you are there are not, they could go after Kurt's family to get to Kurt. His family is probably safer with us there to fight back."

She felt herself feeling weaker and weaker. "I am so tired. I think I will try to sleep again," she said, and within a few minutes she fell fast asleep. Steve looked at his daughter, her neck bandaged, an IV in her arm, dark circles under her eyes, while the rest of her skin was so pale that she hardly looked herself. He shuddered to think of what she'd gone through, and realized that she had asked questions about what they had done and what had happened to everyone else, but had not talked much about what she had been through. Over the years he had seen too many people go through bad trauma to not know the effect it has on the psyche. She would need time, and she would need to be able to talk it out. He remembered when Sandi died. She didn't talk about her mom for almost a year; she had bottled it all up inside for a long time.

Over the next few days, Sara was never left alone, between Steve and Kurt and Zeus, one or more was always at her bedside. Sara was napping on the third day; Steve was sitting in the corner reading a magazine when Aunt Ellie breezed in. Steve steeled himself when he heard her voice in the hall just before she appeared. "For the life of me, child, your father and his escapades will be the death of you. I'll get you home where you can be properly taken care of as soon as they release you," she shrilled.

Sara opened her eyes and blinked, hoping the vision of her aunt might vanish. Her aunt had never frightened her, but the mere thought of being taken from Dad and Kurt was almost her undoing at that moment.

"Excuse me, you know that father you speak of is sitting right here," Steve spoke quietly. "And I would think if you are so concerned about her health, you would at least check to see if she was sleeping when you breezed in here."

"I didn't see you lurking in the corner," she huffed.

Steve shook his head. No matter what anyone said, his sister could and would always turn it around to be someone else's fault. "Ellie, that's enough. I won't have it right now. Sara is too ill to be subjected to your asinine comments. You can either leave or just go to the cafeteria. I'll find you there when Kurt gets here in a few minutes."

For once his sister did not argue. She just turned in a huff, shoving her husband and son in front of her as they headed down the hall. Her voice carried back to the room as she hurried away. "Well, I never. . ."

Sara closed her eyes again, and whispered, "Thank you, Daddy."

"Don't worry, she won't be back. I'll make sure of it," he stated calmly.

Chapter Eighteen

Sara stopped running, barely able to catch her breath. *This infection has really kicked my butt*, she thought. *I used to run five miles and not feel winded. Now I can't even run a mile.* Zeus stopped beside her and barked at Kurt, who was up ahead.

Kurt stopped and turned back quickly. Some days Sara did better than others; today was not one of the better days. "You okay?" he asked, coming back to her.

"Yeah, I just can't breathe. I'm sorry, I can't do anymore today."

"No need to feel sorry. You have a long ways to come back. That infection almost killed you. I'm just glad you are getting better."

"I know, but we agreed, I had to get enough strength back to run a couple of miles before we talk about getting married, and taking a trip to Texas to talk to your family."

"That was your idea," he reminded her. "I don't care if I have to carry you up the aisle. I want you to be my wife, for better or for worse. "He saw the depressed look on her face. "You are getting better all the time. There is no rush or timeline. We are together, I'm here, and I'm not going anywhere."

Between Steve and Kurt, Sara had not been left alone since she was rescued, and if you counted Zeus, she didn't even shower alone. He would not go anywhere without her once she came home from the hospital. He followed her from room to room, and when he could he would lay touching her.

"Dad told me he has an offer to sell Grandpa's ranch, and he said he found a place to move the horses to down near your family's ranch in Texas. I guess the foreman and most of the employees are willing to move." She was still puffing but was trying to change the subject. "You know, I always knew the ranch was there, but I never took the time to think about it much. Dad kept it successfully working all these years so I would have something of Mom's. I always loved it there; it was peaceful. I remember sitting on the porch with my grandpa, rocking in the chairs, watching the foals play in the pasture."

"Does it help to know that our house on the ranch has a big porch? I will make sure we get the rocking chairs, and you can sit in your grandpa's chair and watch the foals in the pasture out front."

She smiled at him. His eyes shone with love. "You are too good to me, Kurt. Thank you; that would be wonderful."

"I talked with my mom today. You know she knew your mom by reputation and her horse, Rapscallion, right?" Sara nodded. "Mom bought one of his foals, and I guess there are a few descendants of his hanging out at the ranch. How's that for a small world?"

"Oh wow, he was quite a horse. He got colic and died a few months after mom died. Grandpa said he died of a broken heart; he missed Mom." A tear traced its way down her cheek. She wiped it away. "Sorry, I miss her too."

"Hey, I get it." He took her in his arms and held her. There was nothing he could say to take away her pain. "I'm sorry; maybe I shouldn't have said anything."

"No, no, it's not that. I am just tired of being tired, and I am really tired of feeling weak." He waited for her to go on, but she just shrugged and said, "Come on, let's go back."

Kurt knew the signs. Sara had yet to talk about her kidnapping and all she had gone through. He knew she had nightmares and was not sleeping well, but she still flatly refused to talk about it. Steve had said, "'Give her time'.", Kurt hoped he was right.

Kurt had met guys coming out of combat, some hurt physically and some not, but mentally, the things they had seen, the experiences, left many of them unable to handle day-to-day life the way they had before. Some found comfort in a bottle, some with drugs, and others became so hooked on the adrenaline of battle that they kept looking for another way of getting that high. He had his own issues; a couple of times, guys in his unit had been killed or maimed in action. Years before he became a SEAL, when he was really little, he had tried to talk to his grandpa about the war he had been in. His grandpa told him that those memories were put away, the good ones and the bad ones, and he tried not to take them out. His grandpa had said, "You can't change them ole memories.

You can't bring back the dead or redo anything you did wrong, so just put the memories away and leave them go. Turn the page and just try to do good in life."   Kurt didn't know if the old man was right or wrong, but he tried to do the same. He thought about how hard some of the spouses had it when their loved ones came home.   Watching someone you love struggle was its own special torture.   Hopefully all Sara needed was time to put her memories away, to move forward and "'do good in life'," but whatever she needed, he wanted to be there for her.

Chapter Nineteen

The first time Sara saw the ranch that was to be her future home, she was almost overwhelmed. Kurt had the exact opposite of her. While she had almost no family, and he had what felt like a half a town's worth. Besides his mother and father, there were two brothers and one sister. His older brother and sister were both married, and there were several kids running around. And then there were a few cousins and a host of employee's and their families, all of whom seemed to be treated like family and all of whom were there to welcome her and Kurt when they arrived.

Then, of course, there were the town's people. Kurt's family had been a part of the small town since its inception in the 1800's. Kurt was considered a hometown hero, and as such, many from the town showed up for his homecoming as well.

She didn't think there was any way to remember all the names, much less who was related to whom.

"Don't worry." Kurt wrapped his arm protectively around her shoulders. "I've been away for awhile. They just want to see the beauty that stole my heart. They won't bite; they are just good, down-to-earth, hardworking people. Look at Zeus—he's checking out the kids."

She looked at Zeus, standing perfectly still while a couple of the kids knelt down around him and petted him. "Good boy, Zeus." She turned to Kurt. "More like the kids are checking out Zeus."

"Is that is his name, Zeus? What a cool name. Does he do tricks? Will he bite? Does he herd cattle? My dad has a cattle dog. My name is Tim. Mom calls me Timmy, and so does Dad, but I like Tim." He stuck out his hand to shake hers.

Sara smiled and shook his hand. "I'm Sara. Let me see if I can answer all those questions. Yes, his name is Zeus, and he shakes hands and fetches, and he will seek out and find things on command. As far as herding cattle, I don't know if he has ever even seen a cow, so he probably doesn't know how to herd them, and yes, he will bite, but only on command. He is very well behaved."

Sara looked up to see her dad walking toward them. "Dad?" was all she said before Tim took over the conversation again.

"That's your dad? He is so cool. He taught me how to shoot a bow and arrow last time he was here, and he went fishing with us down at the pond and jumped off the pier too." The admiration in his voice was palpable. "You know he was a Navy SEAL just like my uncle Kurt?"

Sara laughed; she could not help herself. "Yes, I know he was a Navy SEAL, and you know what else? He taught me how to shoot a bow and arrow too, and how to fish and shoot a gun and a whole lot of things."

Little Tim's eyes widened in surprise and awe. "He did?"

"He did," she responded. "Would you mind showing me around, helping me get to know everyone? I'll bet you not only know everyone, but you know a little something about each one too, don't you?" She asked, thinking that if nothing else, having little Tim as a friend was going to make living here fun! It had been four months since her kidnapping, and it was the first time she'd felt like laughing. Kurt and Steve both noticed, and both breathed a sigh of relief.

The bar-be-cue was not like anything Sara had ever experienced. Not only were there people everywhere, there was food and more food; beef and pork and chicken. People visited and laughed and danced to music playing in the background. It was a huge outdoor party, with kids running all around and everyone doing their best to welcome her and Kurt.

It was late the following afternoon before Kurt and Sara could spend some time with his parents. Sara was adamant they be made aware of the situation. Kurt had not really thought it was all that necessary, but Sara would not accept them not knowing.

"So you think this family in Mexico hates you so much they might try to hunt you down here?" his father asked her. She loved listening to him talk; he had a soothing, measured way of talking.

Kurt answered for her. "We don't know, Dad. We only know what they have done in the past, and considering Alexandro's papa was killed when he kidnapped Sara, I don't think they will suddenly think of us as friends. Sara and I are not looking for trouble. I will do damn near anything to keep her safe, and I think she will be safer here with all of us than anywhere else. But, Sara wanted to be sure you knew the situation. Steve, her dad, and I both feel that if they really wanted to get to me, they would have come here already to hurt me through you."

"It appears that you have thought a lot about this." His father spoke slowly, like he was choosing his words with care. "I know you faced evil people when you were away; I am sorry that you have to face them here. We have been having a lot of problems down here with the cartels and the ones they call coyotes. They are bringing people across the border by the hundreds. Cattle rustling has always happened, but it was never a big problem for us until the last couple of years. Now, we have to constantly be on watch; no one leaves the homestead area unarmed." He looked back at Sara. "I am glad your papa is going to be working with the Cattlemen's Association. I have heard he has some good ideas and the skills to find these bastards!"

"Harry, language!" Kurt's mom intervened.

"Sorry, it is a sore subject. I, for one, am going to be very happy to have you both here. Get married here, as soon as you want to. Kurt, you and Sara come home. Come home, son! We need and want you here with us."

"Thanks Dad; thanks Mom!" Kurt squeezed Sara's hand.

"Thank you both; I was worried what you would think." Sara felt tears burning her eyes. She was touched. These people had raised the love of her life, and she knew without a doubt she was going to be happy here with all of them.

"I want to show you something. I have something for you," Kurt's mom, Marie, stated matter-of-factly. "Come, please, let me show you."

They all rose and followed her out the back door of the house to a small pasture a short distance away. Kurt had an idea of what his mom had planned.

Marie pointed out into pasture, where a beautiful copper-colored mare was grazing. "Rashida," she called. "Rashida, come here, girl." The mare lifted her head, nickered once, and then trotted over to the fence.

"Sara, this is Rashida, and I hope you will accept her as a wedding present from me. She is just a baby, three years old, but I have seen pictures of your mama's horse, Rapscallion, and she looks just like him, except of course she is a she and not a stallion," Marie added laughing. "She is Rapscallion's great-great-granddaughter. Please say you will accept her."

Sara was completely overwhelmed. "Of course. I love her

already. I would be honored." That was all she could stammer out without breaking down crying.

Chapter Twenty

The next morning they were packing to head back to California. There was a lot to do to prepare not only for a wedding but also moving across the country. Kurt's dad yelled out to him that he had company.

"Who now?" Kurt muttered under his breath as he walked to the door. "Come on, sweetheart. Whoever it is will definitely want to meet you too."

"Don't sound so excited," she teased him. "All the packing and moving and hubbub of the wedding will soon be over, and then our lives will settle down."

"Ha," he muttered. They had spent most of the morning explaining that they did not want a huge wedding, while his mother spent most of it explaining about all the people who would need to be included in the festivities.

"Smile, dear. We will figure it out." She kissed him on the cheek and he immediately felt better, though a little guilty for being a short-tempered grouch.

"Sorry, babe. You're right! We will figure it out." He hugged her close as they walked into the living room.

"Figure what out?" a leather-faced man who looked like he had just stepped out of the 1880's asked.

"Uncle Luther. Wow, you look great. Sara; Uncle Luther, a.k.a. the sheriff of Caldina, Texas. Uncle Luther, Sara, the love of my life, soon to be my wife."

"I heard a little about you. Met your papa the other day; he seems pretty proud of you two." He extended his hand and gave hers a firm shake before turning back to Kurt."

"Sorry I missed the bar-be-cue shindig the other day. I had some sheriffin' that had to be done. Wanted to come by and see you and meet the future missus."

"Is everything okay?" Sara asked, almost knowing by the look on his weathered face that it was not.

"Well. . ." He paused. "Before your young man went away to serve his country, he talked to me about becoming a deputy, maybe taking on my job when I was ready to retire."

"That was before—" Kurt started to protest, when Sara interrupted.

"Really? He would make a fantastic sheriff, or deputy," she added, before turning to Kurt and asking, "Why didn't you tell me?"

"After all that's happened since we met, really?" he returned.

"It's kinda important that we talk about it," Luther added. "I am looking at having to retire in the next few months, maybe six on the outside."

"Why?" Kurt asked. "You have been sheriff for as long as I can remember. Are you being forced out?"

"Nah, nothing like that. I have the "'C'" word. Need to get treatment, and I've heard it won't be pleasant."

"I am so sorry, Uncle Luther. Can I call you that?" Sara asked.

"Of course, my dear, I would be honored." He responded, genuinely touched by her. He could see what Kurt saw in her.

"Sara and I will definitely talk about it, Uncle Luther, but really, after all that has happened—"

"Kurt, if that is what you wanted to do, we don't need to talk about it. I think you would be great," Sara interrupted him again.

Kurt turned to his uncle. "You heard her, but we will talk about it, and I will call you in the next couple of days and let you know for sure, one way or the other."

"Just so you know, the county board is in favor of appointing you until the next election. This family has been doing the law enforcement for this county for nearly a hundred years now. I would truly hate to see anyone else in this office. Hell, even my deputies are in favor of you."

They talked for only a short while longer before Marie and Harry came in and the talk turned to ranching and the upcoming wedding.

It was several hours before they got back to their packing, and neither brought up the reason for Luther's visit until they boarded the plane for California the next morning.

"What makes you think I would be a good sheriff?" Kurt asked her after they got settled in their seats, Zeus taking an aisle seat, sniffing each passenger that passed, making many of them a little nervous, while Sara took the center and Kurt the window.

"You need to ask? You just would. You are calm, you are watchful, and you just get things done. Another reason, if you need one, is that if our friends from down south start anything, how much better position would we be in with you in law enforcement?"

"What about you?" he asked.

"What about me?"

"Sara, you are still having nightmares. You are not over your kidnapping. As sheriff there will be plenty of nights that I will be away sheriffin', as Luther calls it. I won't be there for you."

"Then I will just have to deal with it. Seriously," she added when he raised his eyebrows in disbelief. "I have to, Kurt. I am not going to let what happened to me ruin my life. I am going to move forward, and so should you!"

"Says the lady that just told me that it would better if I had an inside track should our 'friends' show back up."

"I said I was going to live my life, but I am not going to run around with blinders on. I don't think I will ever not be watchful. Tell you what, why don't you ask your dad and my dad, see what they say?"

"Okay, that's not a bad idea. Somehow I think your papa is going to agree with you!"

Chapter Twenty-One

The following weeks were extremely busy with, packing, not only the beach house but also her grandparents' home. It was hard to decide what to take and what to dispose of, especially when it came to things that were her mother's. Even though she was exhausted at the end of every day, nightmares still plagued her sleep. She didn't really understand why. During the day, she was not terribly bothered with the memory of the kidnapping .Only when she heard certain sounds or if she got cold did it trigger thoughts during her waking hours, but at night she could not seem to keep the memories at bay.

While cleaning out a closet that was once her mother's, she found a beautiful dress safely stored in the back. As soon as she saw it, she knew it was the dress her mom had worn when she and her dad were married.   Sara remembered seeing a picture of the two of them. She could not resist the urge to try it on.   It was not a fancy dress, definitely not what most would consider a wedding dress, a pale blue jersey that clung to every curve and fit her perfectly. *What will Dad think?*   Was the first thing that came to her mind.   As she stood there in front of the mirror, she twirled around to come face-to-face with her dad.

Seeing the stricken look on his face, she immediately apologized. "I am so sorry, Daddy."

He quickly recovered. "No reason to be sorry. I did not even know she had kept that dress. It brought back some memories, that's all. It looks beautiful on you."

"Why did she wear this dress? It doesn't look like a wedding dress?"

"It was all she had with her when we got married. We were really rushed; she didn't have time to shop. I thought she made a beautiful bride in it."

Sara wasn't sure if she should ask or not but decided it was what she wanted; it would be like her mother was with her." Daddy, can I wear it, as my wedding dress? Would it bother you?"

"I can't say it would bother me. I am sure it will bring back some memories, but I am even surer of one other thing; if your mom were here, she would be over the moon that you want to wear it."

"Thank you, Daddy." She threw her arms around his neck.

Steve wrapped his arms around his daughter, hiding his face from her, afraid she would misunderstand the tears in his eyes. He missed Sandi more right then than he had in quite a while.

"Daddy, why have you never remarried?"

He looked at her a little stunned; she had never asked him anything like that, ever. He walked her over so they could sit on the side of bed. "Your mother was literally the love of my life. I occasionally over the years met women that I thought maybe, maybe I could feel something for, but the thought of another woman raising you, I just couldn't. You are so very much like her. You are, your mother's daughter—strong, yet loving, supportive and capable, and you never shy away from the difficult." He smiled. "Sometimes stubborn; I see her in you nearly every day. I did not want another woman to interfere with your development."

"Wow, I should have asked about her more."

"Why haven't you?" he asked, genuinely wanting to know.

"I never wanted to hurt you and bring up the subject that brought you pain."

"I'm sorry, honey. There is no pain in the memory of your mom. I miss her, I wish we'd had more time, but anytime you want to talk about her, just ask. And I guarantee she would have been very happy that you are wearing her dress."

"Good, I have just one more question today. I found her diaries, there are a few of them; do you care if I read them? Not now, things are too chaotic, but later, I could maybe get to know her better?"

"Wow." He shook his head. "I had no idea all this stuff was still here. Now that I think about it, I don't know where it would've gone, but no, honey, I don't care if you read them. Just don't get rid of them. I'll keep them if you don't want to."

She hugged him and prayed that wearing the dress really would not bother him.

She seemed to still be bothered by something. "What's wrong?" he asked.

"I don't know; pre-wedding jitters? I just keep wondering if I am doing the right thing."

Steve looked at her with furrowed brows. "I don't understand; you love Kurt, right?"

"Yes, with all my heart, but all this—you are giving up your business, your house; dang it, you spent thousands of dollars on my education, and I am throwing it all away to go to the middle of nowhere in West Texas." Steve let her rant uninterrupted, recognizing the fear in her voice. "I am not even sure they have decent internet access. What is a cyber-security tech going to do in the middle of nowhere?

Do they even have computers on the ranch? Kurt will be off being a sheriff, and I will be on a ranch, keeping house and riding my beautiful Arab mare. Am I crazy?"

He hugged her close. "Nope, you are not crazy. You are a little frightened of the unknown maybe. Have you said anything to Kurt about how you feel?"

She shook her head. "If he thought for one second that I might be unhappy, he would say; we stay here. Daddy, we are from different worlds. He has this huge family and friends, and me, I have you, just you and me. I sound like I'm feeling sorry for myself, don't I? I'm sorry, I just . . . I just don't know if this is what I should do."

"Sara, first of all, you need to tell Kurt what you are afraid of, let him know you want to do something besides being a stay-at-home housewife. It's important he knows that you are just like your mother was." He held up his hand." Secondly, I am sure they have computers on the ranch. It is way too big and complicated a business to not have them in today's world. Thirdly, the town has computers and they have computer crime.   And lastly your husband is going to be the sheriff who will have to investigate those crimes. Want me to keep going?"

She shook her head." Sorry, I really didn't think about all that. Instead I was acting like a spoiled little girl."

He hugged her and jokingly said, "I beg your pardon. I did not spoil my daughter!"

"Thanks, Daddy," she whispered.

He knew there was more, that she was not telling him everything, and he was pretty sure she wasn't telling Kurt either. He just hoped she would work it all out sooner rather than later.

The days flew by, and soon Kurt, Sara, and Zeus boarded a plane for the last flight to Texas. They were to be married in a week. Steve would be flying out the next day. The moving vans were finishing packing up, the horse vans had left the day before, and Steve was meeting with Rick, his second-in-command in the business. Rick was going to take over control and eventually buy Steve out.

Part of him would miss the day-to-day challenges of the business, but all of him wanted to be near enough to Sara and Kurt to be a part of their lives and to be able to be a hands-on grandpa. He had encouraged Kurt to take over as sheriff. He was still worried about Sara, but he knew there was nothing either of them could do to help her except to just be there when she needed them.

Chapter Twenty-Two

Sara looked critically at the image in the mirror. She still had not gained back all the weight she had lost when she was sick, and no amount of makeup seemed to hide the dark circles that still showed under her eyes. Before getting to Texas she had worked out every morning, practicing her self-defense, trying to take long runs on the beach, but here it was a little harder to accomplish, so she had taken up riding Rashida in the morning. The little mare was proving to be of a sweet disposition, and she seemed to love her and Zeus. When she would turn her out to pasture after their rides, Rashida and Zeus would often play for a few minutes together. This morning's ride had not been as calming as normal. They were to be married in a short time, and not for the first time she wondered if she would be a good wife. There was no doubt she loved Kurt, but ever since the kidnapping, she seemed to freeze up when they started to become intimate. Kurt never pushed the subject. Instead he told her not to worry, that he wasn't going anywhere, and they had all the time in the world. *But how long can he wait and be put off*, she asked herself. *You have to get past this*, she scolded herself, *Kurt did nothing wrong and was not responsible!*

Marie knocked softly on her door before entering. "Oh my, you look so beautiful, my dear. I have to admit that dress looks fabulous on you."

There had been several discussions about the dress, Marie thinking she should wear a more traditional wedding dress, that Kurt might be disappointed, until finally Sara confronted him and told him what she intended to wear. He supported her without the slightest hesitation. "Are you kidding? That's great; at least you will have something of your mom's besides her saddle." His words did comfort her, but she was still plagued with whether or not she would be a good wife.

"Thank you, Marie. I think I am getting the jitters, and I can't lean on Kurt just yet."

"Soon, my dear, soon, and don't worry, you can lean on me until your papa gets here to walk you down the aisle." She hugged Sara close until she relaxed.

The entire backyard of the main house on the ranch had been transformed with flowers, and chairs, a flower-covered altar at the gazebo, and even a dance floor that had been laid out for the reception. *So much for a small wedding*, Sara thought. As her father walked her out, she saw the large crowd waiting for them. The homecoming bar-be-cue seemed small by comparison. Little Timmy stood right up and gave her a big thumbs-up, bringing a smile to her face.

"Deep breaths, Sara, deep breaths. You'll be fine," Steve quietly encouraged her.

There were a few whispers, and then oohs and aahs, when Zeus calmly walked on Sara's left while Steve was on her right. When the murmurs started, Kurt, who was standing by the altar, turned. His look was enough to make her straighten her back. She thought, *He loves me and he wants to be my husband. One way or another, I will be the best wife possible.*

When they reached the front, Steve, shook Kurt's hand and said, "I know you love and care for my daughter. I can see by the way you look at her, and I know she wants to be your bride and be by your side. Just know that you are now also my son. I love you both." Then Steve turned and walked to a waiting chair. The tears in his eyes welled and rolled down his cheeks. Silently he added, *I did it, Sandi. I got our girl raised. I hope I did you proud.*

Wish you were here with us, honey. I miss you.

There were tears welling up in Sara's eyes when she looked into Kurt's. "I love you, Sara Hoyt. Let's do this." She could only nod and smile, as she took his extended hand.

It was all a blur. She could barely remember saying "I do" until the pastor said, "I now pronounce you husband and wife. Ladies and gentlemen, Mr. and Mrs. Rutledge. Oh, and you may kiss the bride."

There were cheers and laughter as they kissed passionately before walking arm in arm back down the aisle together, Zeus calmly looking on and following them.

They laughed and cheered and joked with all their friends and family. She danced with her father and then her father-in-law while Kurt danced with his mother before the two of them passed them off to each other for their first dance together as husband and wife. She thought it had been a perfect wedding. She had the perfect husband, and he had a wonderful family; they were now her family. All in all, she couldn't have asked for a more perfect day.

They were making their way around the floor for the second time, with Kurt encouraging the other guests to join in, when he saw Luther approaching, and he didn't look happy.

Kurt stopped mid-dance. "What's wrong, Luther?"

"I hate doing this, son, but I need to steal some of your guests."

"Why, what's going on?"

"Three young girls have gone missing. They were supposed to be on a picnic out by the river, for one of their birthdays. When they didn't come home their parents tried calling them. The calls went directly to voicemail. The dad's went to the river. There ain't no sign of the girls. We need to get search and rescue going and see if we can find them. I'm so sorry son."

Sara felt like someone had kicked her in the stomach. Kurt felt her grip tighten on his arm, and he looked at her stricken face. She nodded, before turning to Luther. "Whatever we can do; I will go get changed."

"Sara?" Kurt questioned.

"No worries, there are kids out there that need us. I'll be fine. I will get changed and do whatever I can to help." She looked at Luther." Have you tried to get their phones turned back on? Maybe we can use GPS to see where they are?"

Luther looked at her. "If you can get that handled, it would be a big help, I'll leave Lisa with you; she's one my deputies. If it works, you can send us in the right direction."

"All the money Dad spent on my college degree in computer science and computer security, I can get that done unless the batteries are dead."

She heard Luther making an announcement at the microphone as she left to change. Steve walked over to Kurt. "How is she?"

"I'm not sure." He shook his head. "She said she would be fine. She is going to try to turn the girls' phones back on and get a location on them. One of the deputies is going to stay and help her. You want to come with us?"

Steve thought for a moment then replied, "Absolutely!"

Chapter Twenty-Three

Sara changed quickly, forcing her mind to stay calm and focused; she grabbed her laptop and walked out the door. A young deputy was waiting for her. "I'm Lisa. Luther told me to help you in any way you needed to get into the girl's' phones. Not sure what you or how you do that, but I'm here. Just tell me what to do."

"Can you get me the phone numbers and the carriers? I'll need you to use your badge number to get the carriers to turn them on. From there I should be able to patch into them and get a fix on where they are. I can do all that from right here at the ranch. We have decent cell service close to the house. It gets a little spotty away from here."

"I got that information while you were changing; I wasn't sure what else you would need. I didn't even know we could do that."

Sara smiled, taking the paper Lisa held out to her with the numbers on it. "There are things that can be done with cell phones that are actually pretty scary now days. In order to do cyber-security, you basically learn how to be a hacker; cell phones are nothing more than portable computers. Honestly with the right equipment we don't have to get the carriers to help us, but it's better if we do."

Sara made a few calls. Within a couple of minutes she had found the correct person, and they verified that they were allowed to turn on the phones. From there, it was only a few minutes until she could see the phone locations.

"Ah. . . Lisa, can you come over here?" Sara asked.

"What's up, can you see them?" Lisa asked as she came closer.

"Yes, but they are nowhere near where we thought," Sara said, quietly so no one could overhear her.

"What? Where are they?"

"Quiet. Let's not panic anyone. Let's just tell them we are going to follow up on a lead and get out of here."

"Okay. . ." Lisa said, and then added hesitantly, "So what's the matter? They aren't where we thought, but we know where they are, right?"

They got into Lisa's squad car, a 4 x 4 Ford Explorer. Zeus jumped into the back seat. "We'll let you know what we find!" Lisa called out to the few people standing around the reception area. Most of the men, teenagers, and young women had headed out to help with the search, while anyone left was cleaning up the food and gathering the small children and keeping them entertained.

"Alright, spill it. What's going on? And, ah, where are we going?" Lisa asked, driving out the driveway.

"Toward Austin, the phones look like they are about an hour out, and they are moving fast."

"Really? Then we need to get everyone headed that way, call the girls, and let them know we are on to them.""

Sara shook her head. "What if they have been kidnapped? If we call, then the kidnappers could react badly, especially if the girls told them they didn't have phones, or if they are running away, they might throw the phones out and we lose the ability to track them. It's too risky until we get eyes on them. I think we should tell Luther and Kurt what we know; their phones are on the way to Austin. We do not know if the girls even have their phones. For all we know, they could be stranded out there in the middle of nowhere and someone else has their phones."

Lisa shook her head. "Okay, I didn't think of that; and I should have. You get in touch with Luther, and I will put pedal to the metal."

Lisa drove as fast as possible out the long, graveled road to the highway while Sara called Luther and Kurt and gave them an update.

"We'll get the Rangers involved and see if they can help get eyes on the car. You guys try to catch them, code 3, and if they are being held we can throw out on the wires as a possible 207." Luther shook his head, turning to Kurt and Steve. "This is not looking good, guys. Those girls' phones are halfway to Austin. We just don't know if they are with them or the girls are stranded out here somewhere."

Steve and Kurt looked at each other. After their last experience with Sara, they both were thinking the worst, and they both were wondering how Sara was handling things. Kurt was the first to reply. "Let's split up, chances are the girls are with their phones and not here. We haven't seen any sign of them. But just in case, let's leave the guys searching here and grab Harry Stein's chopper and make tracks to Austin. Harry still has a chopper, doesn't he?"

"Yep, but Harry's out of town; either one of you know how to fly a chopper?"

"I do," Kurt replied.

"Yes," Steve added.

"Alright then, I'll let Sadie, Harry's wife know and we will get going." Luther agreed.

By the time they got to the chopper, fueled it up, and got all set, it was a full thirty minutes before they were airborne. During that time Sara and Lisa were flying down the highway, lights and sirens blazing.

Lisa noticed how quiet Sara was. She was constantly checking the computer to follow the girl's' phones, but other than occasionally letting her know they were on the right track, she barely spoke. "I heard about you, ya know," Lisa said. "Is it true or just a nasty rumor?"

"That I was kidnapped?" Sara asked without emotion.

"Yes; I just want to know if you are going to be all right?"

"I am going to be fine so long as we can find these girls alive and well. If not, I am probably going to be a complete mess," Sara admitted.

"I just want to know what I'm facing if we get there and they are kidnapped. I also heard you are pretty versed in self defense, and the use of a gun. Are you going to be able to back me up or. . .?" Lisa let the question go unfinished.

"Don't worry about me; if they have been kidnapped, however, you might say a prayer for whoever is holding them if I get to them first," Sara joked.

"Okay then." Lisa picked up on the lighter tone. "Good to know!"

Luther had called the Rangers, who sent a car to try to intercept the girl's' car without actually stopping them. The Rangers were sure it was runaways, so they didn't think it was all that big a deal.

Sara had gone through one girl's emails and texts on her phone and had not found anything suspicious, but when she got to the next phone, her fears were confirmed. "They are being lured to a mall called The Shops; they are meeting a guy near Nordstrom's." Sara's voice was only just loud enough for Lisa to hear, but it was emotionless.

"I know where that is. It's on this side of town."

"It is, and they are almost there. Looks like we are only a few minutes behind them now."

Lisa radioed the Rangers again, and then had dispatch get with mall security. "Tell them to attempt to stall the girls, but approach with care. They could be with someone that is dangerous and possibly armed."

"There." Sara pointed to three black SUV's lined up. There were several girls being ushered toward and into them.

The security guard approached and raised his hand, yelling something; whatever it was caused the wrong reaction. Shots rang out. The girls screamed and scattered in a dozen directions. Sara watched as the guard fell to the ground, obviously hit, and as the Explorer rolled to a stop she was out, gun out, and running straight toward the chaos with Zeus right beside her.

Sara saw the guard on the ground. He appeared to have been shot in the leg. Her eyes scanned the crowd. One man, probably the leader, was holding a girl with a gun in her side; he was backed up against one of SUV's.

She did not see any of the other men that had been with the girls a few moments earlier; she hoped someone would help by catching them.

Sara stopped. Her gun was aimed directly at the kidnapper's head. Everything seemed to slow down. It became quiet, several Ranger vehicles arrived, and those officers were exiting their vehicles, guns drawn and pointed at the kidnapper.

"Let me go and I won't hurt her!" He yelled out. "She is very pretty; it would be a shame for her to get a hole in her head. "The young girl squirmed. She was obviously terrified.

His accent reminded Sara of Salazar. She felt sick to her stomach, but her gun never wavered. "If you shoot her, I will have to shoot you; I don't think you came here to die today. If you put your gun down, you might have to serve some time, but right now nobody has died. You'll be out in a few years."

One of the Rangers started to interrupt, but his partner stopped him. "Let's see how this plays out. She may have this," he whispered. Sara's senses were on high alert; she heard him clearly.

"I think you are bluffing. I don't think you will shoot me while I hold this girl, but I am not bluffing. I can shoot her and hurt her without killing her, or I can kill her. It matters not to me," the kidnapper called out.

"I'm not bluffing," Sara replied. Her voice was calm and cold—no emotion showed." I am an expert with this gun. One shot directly through your throat severs your spinal cord. You will drop, unable to move, but your brain will stay alive for a few minutes. You will know you are dying. The girl, she'll have your blood all over her, but she'll be alive. Now put the gun down and let's all live."

Sara watched as he swallowed nervously, his gun wavered but it was not lowered. Sara's non-emotional, graphic description made him question his power. Zeus growled. He had moved around to only a few feet from the kidnapper, and now was in a crouched position, ready to attack. "I could let Zeus have you. He'll probably only break your arm, and rip it to shreds." She winced. "Painful but not deadly, unless he goes for your throat, that;" she paused, "that will be really ugly. Zeus, back one, please." Zeus slid back one step." As you can see, I can control exactly what he does."

Fear showed in the kidnapper's face now; Zeus was extremely intimidating. "I will shoot him." He started to move his gun to point at Zeus.

"Don't!" Sara called out. "He will attack!" Now the gun was not pointed at either the girl or Zeus; instead, it was frozen somewhere in between. "Just lower the gun and this will all be over. I will call Zeus back."

Slowly the gun lowered, until he dropped it on the ground at his feet. The young girl struggled free and ran off to one side. Several officers rushed in to make the arrest, and Sara called Zeus to her side. She let out a sigh of relief, holstering her gun then leaning forward, hands on her knees, taking deep breaths.

"That was incredible," Lisa said, hurrying up to her side. "Are you okay?"

Sara shook her head. "Yeah, I think so. I'm sure glad I didn't have to shoot him, my hands were not that steady. Thank God he didn't call my bluff."

"I couldn't tell." Lisa laughed. "I have to say, your voice was pretty intimidating. I felt like complying!"

"I have to agree, that was pretty impressive." One of the Rangers had walked up. "I heard Luther was getting some new deputies, but he didn't say he had a badass chick like you."

"That badass chick is my wife," Kurt stated proudly as he walked up. He stuck out his hand toward the Ranger. "Kurt Rutledge,I'm supposed to be replacing Luther in a few weeks as the new sheriff."

"Sam Nixon, Texas Ranger. No disrespect meant, Sheriff. But she was, I don't know, kind of hard to describe. Badass is all that fits."

"I get it. I've seen her in action a couple of times now, and your description is actually pretty accurate."

"When did you get here?" Sara asked Kurt, slowing getting herself calmed down.

"Couple of minutes ago. We landed a chopper over there and came running, just in time to watch the guy put his gun down. Are you all right?"

Kurt asked, wondering if all this would bring back the whole Salazar scene.

"I'm fine." She turned to her father and Luther, who were walking up, and repeated, "I'm fine."

"I never doubted it," Steve replied with a smile." From what I heard walking up, you are; an amazing, incredible, badass chick, and I think a couple more adjectives, I didn't take notes, but I am proud to call you my daughter."

"Thanks, Dad."

"This is going to be a long night. Sorry to ruin your weddin' night," Luther put in, giving Sara a hug. "Hear ya did good, girl. We are all going to be stuck here for a few hours while the parents of all these young ladies get brought in and everyone gets interviewed. I'll get you guys out of here as soon as I can."

"No worries, Luther. We'll be fine," Kurt replied, looking at Sara for confirmation.

"Absolutely; we have a lifetime together; this is only a few hours. What can we do?" Sara asked.

"Gonna be a lot of wait'n. They're gonna setup a couple of meet'n rooms in the mall for us. Might as well make yourself comfortable there, while I school your hubby a little on procedures," Luther replied dryly.

The hours did drag by. Sara was interviewed by several troopers and then by a couple of detectives. By midnight she was feeling pretty exhausted. She decided to take a walk and find Kurt or her dad.

As she was walking out, she saw the girls with their parents all gathered in another room. A trooper stood by the door; many of the voices sounded upset. "Mind if I go in and talk to them?" she asked.

He recognized who she was from earlier. "I don't think anyone would mind." He opened the door for her.

She walked in hearing some parent's' angry voices, others crying. Everyone's emotions were running high. Zeus moved quietly beside her.

Slowly she made her way to the front of the room. One of the girls saw her, and started shushing everyone.

Slowly the room became quiet, and they all looked at her.

"I just want you all to know, to understand, what almost happened today," she stated with a quiet, firm voice. 'To all you parents, you almost lost your daughters. You came very close to never seeing them again, and you would probably never have known what happened to them. You might have thought they ran away. You might never have known they were lured into coming here, and they would have faced unspeakable horrors. They found handcuffs and zip ties in the SUV's. They also found enough Fentanyl, Rohypnol, and Special K to keep a herd of elephants sedated. The girls would have been drugged and raped, and raped and raped again and again and again until they were submissive." Sara heard some of the people reacting in horror as she continued. "And then they would be used as prostitutes or they would have been sold, probably to someone in another country. They would then have been raped and abused by their new owners, until they tired of them, and then they would probably be killed and dumped somewhere. They would never have been seen or heard from again." A few in the room gasped at her description. "You girls, you were lured here by experts. They knew just what to say to get you to come to them, but don't let this experience cripple you from living. Instead, learn from it. Learn self-defense, learn . . . learn from what happened and make sure you don't fall for it again. If you have girlfriends or sisters, make sure you teach them so they don't get lured into a similar trap.

"And finally, love each other. Parents, this is going to be hard, but make sure the girls know that you are there for them. Don't be angry, be grateful. Be grateful that you still have your daughters."

With that, Sara turned to walk out. She had noticed that Kurt and her dad had slipped into the back of the room during her speech.

One girl held up her hand." Can I ask you a question?"

"Of course, what do you want to know?" Sara smiled at her.

"Is it true that you were kidnapped?"

News sure travels fast, Sara thought. She took a deep breath before answering. "Yes, yes, it is true. I was kidnapped about six months ago, and I was lucky my fiancé and father rescued me, but . . . not before I was drugged with a dirty needle and given a staph infection that nearly killed me. Not before I was undressed by I don't know whom and thrown into a ten by ten cage with only my underwear and bra on." Again she heard gasps. "I was left on a cold cement floor. Where there was nothing to sit on except a bucket to relieve myself in. There was no blanket or cot; there was no way to stay warm." Her voice rose some as the memories flooded back; Zeus, sensing her tension, moved closer to her side and touched her leg with his head. She continued, "I was given an apple and a bottle of water one day, and then they gave me a scrap of material to wear. I was told to remove my bra, and put their so-called dress on while they filmed me for an auction. Later I was told that I sold for a hundred thousand dollars." Several more people let out audible gasps. "But let me be clear—in spite of all of that, I consider myself lucky. I was mortified by what happened to me. I was very ill and have not completely recovered my pre-kidnapping strength and stamina, but I am home, and earlier today, I married that fiancé and spent the day while we were supposed to be at our reception and leaving for our honeymoon helping rescue you guys. I can't think of anything more worthwhile to do with our time, than to make sure

you never experience anything like I did.
I thank God I could help stop what was
about to happen. So now I would like to
say goodbye, good luck, and God bless. I
am going to go home with my husband."
She waved her hand at Kurt.

"One more question?" the same
girl asked.

"Sure."

"Were you raped? If so, how did
you get over it?"

Sara looked at the young woman.
Her voice was soft, but firm. "I don't
know if I was raped. I knew who my
kidnapper was, so it would not surprise
me. He was an evil man. I hope I never
meet anyone ever again that is as evil as
he was, but by the time I was rescued
the staph infection had taken over. I

had a lump the size of a tennis ball on the side of my neck. I was running a really high fever and was in and out of consciousness. By the time I was aware of everything it just. . . it just didn't seem important. What was important was I was rescued and in a safe place. And I get up every morning thankful to be alive and safe. I thank God that I am with people who love me."

"That's what's important. I firmly believe you need to learn some sort of self-defense. Learn what to do if you are put in a really bad place. The one regret I have is that I believed my kidnapper when he said that if I went with him willingly, he would not hurt the other hostages he was holding. Instead, he shot several of them. Five died, and more were injured. I regret that I didn't fight back and shoot my way out of the situation and not get taken in the first place. I don't know if I would be alive today or if he would have killed me. We don't always know what to do. But take the time to learn as much as you can about what to do in every situation you can, then pray to God that you make the right move. Thanks for listening."

"Will you teach us? I live in Caldina; I go to school there. Will you teach us self-defense?"

"I will talk with the principal and see what can be arranged. Give me some time; okay?" Sara replied.

"Thank you." The young girl stood up and started clapping; everyone in the room followed suit.

During the exchange Kurt looked ruefully at Steve. "I think we have opened Pandora's Box. With all the press here, she is bound to be recognized."

Steve shook his head. "Yeah, well, she is her mother's daughter; if she can help she is going to jump in with both feet and do one hell of a job. If it wasn't today, it would be tomorrow or next week or next month. We can't stop the storm; we can only batten down the hatches."

Kurt nodded in agreement and walked quietly toward where Sara was standing and led her toward the door.

"I think you were a hit," Kurt whispered in her ear as they slipped out, her father and Zeus close behind.

"Luther is waiting out by the chopper for us."

His breath on her neck sent chills up her spine—not bad chills, good ones, very good ones, Sara realized.

When they arrived at the chopper, Luther was nowhere to be found. They looked around but could not find him." I'll walk back and see if someone held him up."

As he was leaving, a young paramedic ran up." Are you Kurt?"

"Yes, ma'am."

"We have the sheriff in the ambulance. He collapsed, but he won't let us take him to the hospital until he has talked to you."

"Let's go." Kurt headed out with her, Sara, Steve, and Zeus all right behind, Kurt silently asking himself what else could happen today.

Luther was lying on a gurney in the back of the ambulance; his face was pale even with his tanned skin."Sorry, boy. I wanted to hang on until you got back from your honeymoon. I am so sorry."

"Luther, don't worry about it. Hell, we already missed our flight. We're good. What do you need from me?"

Luther looked over at Sara. "I need you to take on the badge now, instead of in a couple of weeks."

"Got it. No worries. You get to the hospital and get treated."

Sara nodded in agreement. "Absolutely, Luther, we will be fine.

Like I said earlier, we have our whole lives ahead, and when you get well, we'll take our honeymoon then." She knew by looking at him that might never happen, and her heart went out to him. The short time she had known Luther, she felt he was like the uncle she never had. She jumped up into the ambulance and kissed him on the cheek. "We will be just fine; we just need you to be just fine!"

"I'll second that," Kurt added while helping Sara back down.

"Here are my keys to the office, and my house. Your badge is in my top right desk drawer. Raise your right hand." Kurt raised his hand. "Do you solemnly swear to uphold the laws of the county of Caldina, and fulfill all the duties of the sheriff of said county?"

"I do," Kurt responded.

"Good. Here's my badge, until you get yours. Can you check on my animals at the house; find someone to take care of them until I get out of the hospital?"

"Of course; don't worry. We'll get over there and get them fed and watered."

Luther took a breath; it seemed like he was getting weaker. "They'll be fine tonight. They are used to me being gone. They know the neighbor; he can introduce you to Wilber, my dog. Oh, and one more thing. Jason called; he's one of the board of supervisors; he said they held an emergency meeting on the phone this evening. After everything that happened today, what you asked for at your interview last week is approved."

Kurt looked at Luther blankly, not immediately remembering what he'd asked for.

"She is approved to be a deputy, a consultant, pretty much whatever you want. They were impressed!"

"Sir, we need to get him to the hospital. His vitals are not looking good."

"Take him. Don't worry about anything, Luther. Just get well."

Nearly two thousand miles away, a lawyer was awakened by a text message on his phone. "Let your client know—we found them."

Chapter Twenty-Four

Sara was surprised Zeus willing followed them into the helicopter. She thought Zeus might object like before but he seemed to accept it so long as they were together. No one had done a lot of talking on the flight back; it was too noisy, but when they landed, Sara said something that stopped them both in their tracks.

They were walking toward Luther's and Kurt's SUVs. Kurt said, "Here, sir, why don't you take my SUV home? Sara and I can take Luther's. We can get everything back where it belongs tomorrow, or later today."

As he handed Steve his keys, Sara spoke. "I want to meet with Salazar's son."

"What?" They both asked in unison.

Kurt added, "Why? What for?"

"I've been thinking about it for awhile now, but after tonight, yesterday." She hesitated. "All that happened, there were news people. The Salazar's are going to know where I am, where we all are. Look, Alexandro is a playboy, at least he always was. Maybe I can talk to him and get him to drop this ridiculous feud."

Steve spoke first. "Sara, you are really tired; we all are. Let's talk about this when we are all more rested."

"I'll second that," Kurt added.

Sara sighed. "Okay, but I'm serious. This is something I really need to do."

Steve sighed, "I don't know where this is coming from, but we will talk about it, soon. Okay? And for the record, I didn't know that you didn't know." She looked at him not understanding. "I thought you knew you were not raped. God knows I thought for sure Salazar would have raped you himself. Paul ordered the doctors to do a rape kit when you were in the hospital; the doctors said there was no sign of rape."

"Thanks Dad, I. . .thanks." She gave him a hug. "Love you! But this is not about that. I'm glad you told me, but this is about our future, all of us."

"Love you too, honey. Just go home, be safe, and we will talk in a few days."

She yawned. "Yes, after a really long nap, okay?"

Kurt and Sara pulled up in front of their house at the ranch a while latter. "Home, babe," Kurt shook Sara awake. "Let's go home."

"Mmmm, that sounds wonderful." Sara cuddled into his arms.

"It does, doesn't it? Sorry about our honeymoon. Had it all planned in the Caribbean—a few islands, white beaches, long nights."

Sara smiled up at him. "Ya know, I heard the Caribbean is highly overrated for newlyweds. A much better location is for them to camp out under the stars in West Texas with a couple of horses and a dog."

"Really?" He smiled down at her. "You sure that wouldn't be a bit of a comedown?"

She shook her head." I just want to be with you no matter where we are, just so long as we are together. Oh, one thing, though, before we count this night finished. What the hell was Luther talking about, 'She's approved'?"

"Oh that." He grimaced in a teasing way. "I sort of told them that if they wanted me, I was a package deal with you, at least as a consultant, preferably as a full-time deputy."

"You what?" She gasped. "What made you think of that?"

"Well, I have seen you in action, and you absolutely proved your worth today, well, yesterday. I want to work with you. Call me crazy, baby. I am crazy, just crazy about you. Did you mean what you said about camping out under the stars?" He changed the subject.

"I did, but considering it is nearly four a.m., I doubt we can get very far now."

"I know a great spot. As soon as things have settled some, we will take the time for a belated honeymoon. Is that the right word, belated, like a belated birthday wish?"

"I'm not sure, but it works for me." Never had she felt so much love for one person as she felt right then at that moment. She knew in her heart that no matter what life had in store, having Kurt by her side would make it complete.

"Come on. This has probably been one of the most unconventional wedding nights ever; no sense in changing things up now. Let's go get some sleep!" And with that, Kurt swept her into his arms and carried her across the threshold into their home, Zeus right behind.

Chapter Twenty-Five

It was late the next morning when she awoke. Kurt stood in the doorway with a tray in his hands, wearing nothing but his boxers." I made you some breakfast. We didn't get much to eat yesterday, and I, for one, woke up as hungry as an old bear just out of hibernation."

She looked up at him, standing and holding the tray with only his boxers on, and a wave of emotion swept over her. "I admit being a little on the ravenous side." She smiled at him. "And while I would enjoy that, maybe food can wait while we do what most couples do on their wedding night?"

He set the tray down on a nearby side table. "The hungry bear can wait," he said with a smile, as he quickly slipped into the bed next to her. His first kiss left her little doubt of his feelings, and hers matched as her body arched into his.

When they both lay replete a short while later, Sara realized she had not thought about her kidnapping once. All she had thought of was how much she loved Kurt and wanted to please him. For his part, Kurt was a kind lover who put her needs far in front of his own.

"Are you okay?" Kurt asked quietly.

"Yes, most definitely," she whispered back.

He did not want to bring up her kidnapping, but he felt like it was still an elephant in the room. "Sara, all that happened yesterday, did it help or . . . ?"

She hesitated. "I think what helped was helping someone else, having the knowledge to save those girls, to be able to tell them not to let it destroy their lives. It helped to realize just how very blessed I am to have you and Dad and your family, especially you. Not many guys would have waited as patiently as you have."

He sighed, "Believe me, it was worth the wait. I cannot imagine my life with anyone else. We are in this together, 'for better or worse' as they said yesterday."

The End

Epilogue

"For No Apparent Reason" will be
coming soon—it is the continuation of
Sara's story, her journey into becoming
a deputy, and the ongoing feud with
Salazar's family.

www.ingramcontent.com/pod-product-compliance
Lightning Source LLC
Chambersburg PA
CBHW050529110726
47899CB00005B/1653